Prolog

"...it seems like everything is dying.
---Karen Young

The air is filled with the sharp scent of wind-swept tree limbs.

Children run through the streets. Their footsteps trample the countless leaves that litter the ground. The breeze carries the leaves and makes them dance around pedestrians. The days are shorter, the nights longer. Nature's colorful spectacle signals the coming changes.

Autumn has arrived in the city of Winsor.

Last Night

Those relationships, these years, this life
Now only exist in your minds
And then no more

"Mr. Winston? Mr. Winston!"

Charles Winston turned at the sound of his name. Right away, a casual observer could see that Charles was not a friendly man. Years of grimaces and disapproving looks had left marks all over his face. His eyesight was terrible, but he refused to wear a pair of eyeglasses; stating that they made him look 'frail' and 'weak'. Two conclusions that an observer would be hard pressed to come by. At just under six feet, he weighed 210 lbs. Though no longer the serious athlete that he was in his high school and college days, he retained a wide, intimidating frame. This frame coupled with his constant squinting, usually mistaken for frowning, gave off anything but the impression of frailty. Or welcoming.

"What is it, Allen?"

Allen Carter was, in most respects, the opposite of Charles. He was somewhat shorter coming in at 5' 8", and just as wide, though Allen only dreamt of having a solid build. Most of his weight, comically, had centered on his torso. Leaving him with a belly that poured over his beltline and a skinny set of legs that seemed disproportioned. He was never seen without a pair of eyeglasses which even he would have to admit made him look frail and weak.

"Mr. Winston, um, we need to talk about the budget."

Charles squinted at him, more so from focusing on his features and less from malevolence as Allen thought. "What of it?"

Allen glanced down at the spreadsheet he had pulled up on his phone. "Well," he started after clearing his throat, "I see on the board that you have the current shoot---"

"The deserted mansion."

"Yes. Right." He adjusted his glasses. "You have it scheduled for a five day shoot."

"That's right. That's what I need."

"Well we...can't...do that."

Charles squinted at Allen again and there was no mistaking the meaning behind it this time. "What the hell is this shit?"

"We---" Allen cleared his throat and wiped his cellphone screen across his pant leg. It was obscured with sweat. "With the greenhouse shoot last week...I'm sure you remember all the issues that came up."

"Yes," he huffed, "I nearly walked out."

"We ended up having to add an additional two shooting days to cover for the lead actress's absence and for the, uh, Landscaping Incident."

'The Landscaping Incident' was merely a small misunderstanding that quickly escalated into a feud between the film director (Charles Winston) and the entirety of Mow Better Landscaping Co.

The current owners of the land where the greenhouse shoot had taken place, after agreeing to allow the film crew to work there for a week, had forgotten to check the schedule for any previous engagements. Specifically, the hiring of Mow Better to come by and work on the area surrounding the old greenhouse. The area where the film crew was set up and working.

What began as a brief conversation of Charles telling the landscapers to 'fuck off' in the politest euphemisms possible rapidly degenerated. Mow Better claimed only the homeowners could tell them that the job was canceled and Charles believed he had equal right to be working there for prepayment of services being rendered. When Charles took a swing at one of the landscapers and had to be held back by two guys from the art department, it was decided to call the day off and get the homeowners involved.

The homeowners backed up the film crew in the debate, but also stated that the crew would never be allowed anywhere near the property again once the shoot was finished.

"None of that could be helped," Charles replied curtly.

"Well," Allen adjusted his glasses again and did his best to meet Charles's gaze, "if we stick to the five day shoot, then we're cutting into all of the remaining shoots. And two of them are the biggest and most expensive ones. Plus, that cuts into any extra days we might need for reshooting."

"Which will be scheduled. I'm not happy with some of the dailies that have been coming back. And I meant to tell you that the other day; I apologize for not getting back to you sooner. We need to get those all worked out."

"And *that*," Allen continued, "is even more of a reason to try and cut this week short and move on to the next shoot. We'll just be making things more difficult on ourselves down the road."

"It's not gonna happen. I'm sorry, but you just need to find a way to get this done. I need that five day shoot, Allen." Then he turned from Allen and began to walk on to the set.

"But---!" Allen called out unintentionally.

Charles turned halfway around with a frown deeply etched into his brow. "Was there something else?"

Allen's eyes flinched away from the piercing stare to the set, his shoes, anywhere other than that face. "No, sir, I'll get it done."

Charles nodded and continued walking away. Allen watched him for a while, and then glanced back at the spreadsheet on his phone, which was now useless. He tucked the phone away in his pocket, adjusted his glasses, then walked away from the set in the opposite direction of Charles.

*   *   *   *   *   *   *   *   *

"He told you *what?*" Dylan yelled, trying to be heard over the bar jukebox.

" 'Get it done' he said. The whole reason I went to him was because I *couldn't* get it done! Now I'm supposed to wave my hand and do magic!" Allen physically demonstrated, spilling a large portion of the beer in his hand on to the counter. He didn't notice.

The Slanted Donkey was a simple bar. 'Simple' in that it only served beer and liquor; no food or snacks. The outside of the building was in serious need of repair, looking on the verge of collapse in several spots. A few tables and a small stage for karaoke rounded out the interior. No bands ever played on the stage; the average turnout was usually only a handful of locals. Allen had asked Dylan to meet him here at the Slanted Donkey after work for a drink. It wasn't that the two of them were very close or that either of them would have even called the other a friend, but Dylan was the only person on the film crew willing to drink with Allen. Allen wasn't obnoxious or rude or demanding; it was simply that most people found him boring. Every time he asked someone out for a drink, they could immediately think of something they would rather do instead. Even if that was nothing more than watching television.

Dylan Haddon didn't care either way, so he found no reason to turn Allen down. He was dressed plainly in a simple black t-shirt, blue jeans and a dark blue hoodie jacket without markings. He always wore a long sleeve shirt or a jacket because he always felt a chill. He was starting to see signs of a receding hairline when he got ready in the mornings, but he decided it was too slight to worry about. If it got bad, he told himself, he would just start wearing caps.

"I think I'm gonna quit."

Dylan turned toward Allen and motioned for him to repeat himself. Couldn't be sure he heard him correctly over the noise.

Allen started to lean towards him. "I said: I think I'm---" He lost his balance and crashed into Dylan, spilling more of the beer. "I'm quitting," he yelled after wiping off the front of his shirt.

"Charles is an asshole. Don't let him get to you."

Allen waved this off then laced his hands together on top of his belly. "It's not just that. I mean...well you know, right? What I'm getting at? I just don't have..." He trailed off looking at the mirror behind the bar and stared at his reflection for a while. "Are you happy? I mean, you have *pride* in what you do?"

Dylan shrugged and took a couple sips of his beer. "I think 'pride' is a strong word for it. I don't *hate* what I do. Never have."

"And that's good enough for you? That's it?"

Now Dylan was starting to regret coming here. "I'm not asking for anything else, Allen. At least I have a job, with decent pay. Not everyone can say that."

Allen sighed and looked away from his reflection. Took off his glasses and wiped his face with one of the small napkins nearby. "I know what you're saying. I'm being selfish, aren't I? Of course I am, I'm sorry. I just feel like...I want..." He threw his hands up and turned to Dylan, pleadingly, as if he could communicate by look alone what he couldn't articulate. "Something's...something's *missing*, you know?"

Dylan nodded, though he had no idea what Allen was going on about. He hoped it didn't show in his features.

Suddenly, Allen stood up, reached into his pocket and placed a dollar bill on the counter. He never once glanced at the amount of it. "Hey," he said while placing his hand on Dylan's shoulder, "thanks for meeting me here. I just needed to---I needed this." Then he patted him on the shoulder and began walking toward the exit.

Dylan felt the hairs on the back of his neck stand up. Something seemed strange about the tone of Allen's words, but he couldn't place it. "Hey, Allen?" he called out. He was certain that Allen wouldn't be able to hear him over the music, but after placing his hand on the doorknob, he turned back toward him. Dylan paused, then stated simply, "I'll see you at the office tomorrow."

Allen gave a thin, sad smile, then a small wave and walked out of the bar.

Dylan continued to look at the exit doors long after Allen had left. The beer in his hand all but forgotten.

This night, it turned out, was the last time he saw Allen Carter alive.

Sleep, Dear One

Did you hear me calling?
While you were asleep?
I tried to reach you
But you were immersed
In your dreams deep

Do you feel the rain falling?
Do you feel the dirt?
Let me know if you're uncomfortable
If this makes you scared
Or if it hurts

Sleep, dear one
Sleep, and be brave
I must return now
I'm so exhausted
From digging your grave

    Karen Young inhaled deeply from the cigarette. She started the motions toward rising, but immediately she let her muscles go slack and stayed seated.
    Couldn't do it. She still couldn't do it.
    She was seated on the front steps leading up to Hill First Baptist Church. The day was warm and clear and the wind was very chilly. She was wearing a small black jacket with a matching skirt and shoes. Each time the wind picked up, she regretted not wearing slacks. Her hair was light brown with remnants of blonde dye spread throughout. She had been meaning to get her hair touched up, but didn't have a chance to as of yet. The cigarette was shaking in her fingers, but not from the cold.
    She remembered the first funeral she had been to. Her great aunt on her mother's side passed away when she was eight. Lost a long, hard battle with breast cancer. The small silver lining was that she died peacefully and with a smile on her face.
    Karen remembered sitting in the service and spending the entire time feeling like a spectator. She watched as family members and friends of the family wiped their eyes, spoke of cherished moments and memories, and took long solemn gazes at the casket in

front of them. She didn't feel like a participant because she didn't feel anything.

The body laid out in front of her, which she had interacted with on many occasions throughout her life, now seemed to be nothing more than another decoration in a room full of them. People took turns walking over to the casket and peering inside. A shake of the head, a dab at the eyes with a handkerchief or a deep sigh were the repeated reactions. Once they had moved on, the participants spoke compliments about the deceased.

Karen spent her time watching. She felt as strong of an attachment to the body of her great aunt as she would to a complete stranger. It wasn't as if she didn't accept or understand what had happened. It was instead as if it simply didn't matter.

The next funeral she experienced happened during senior year of high school. Sarah Kinnely, age 17, and her boyfriend Josh Mason, age 18, were both killed in a car crash. The details of the accident were sketchy at first, but some believed it was yet another result of drunk driving. The principal made the announcement over the intercom on the day the news broke.

At first there was a streak of disbelief that spread throughout the school. Was this a prank? Was the faculty trying to send a message? As it became apparent that the announcement was nothing but fact, a stronger sense of disbelief that veered toward anger flowed through Karen. How could this be possible? She had just seen Sarah *yesterday*. It was as if such a short time span made a difference. If it were several months, a year...but *yesterday?*

Karen refused to believe it until the moment she stood above Sarah's casket. It was a closed casket service; there was no possible way for it to be otherwise. When she stood over it, surrounded by flowers and saw the wreath off to the side with an enlarged version of Sarah's yearbook photo in the middle, she began to shake.

It began with her hands, then quickly spread to her legs. She was surprised to find herself seated on the floor in the middle of a ring of people. Two people had their hands on her arms, holding her in place. Could she stand? Could she walk? She made an attempt and fell immediately back to the ground.

She couldn't do it.

Three years ago, she lost both of her grandmothers roughly around the same time. One suffered from dementia along with failing health. She died in a hospital bed, screaming out the name of her husband, who had been dead well over a decade prior.

The second went as ideally as death could be. She started to have issues with exhaustion; no matter how much she slept, it never seemed to be enough. One day, shortly before lunchtime, she told her husband that she was going to lie down for a few minutes. He kissed her on the forehead and told her he'd check in on her shortly. She went to sleep with a book on her chest and the cold winter sun pouring in through the window. She never woke up.

This year, she lost a cousin to a brain tumor. While they never spoke very often over the years, she still felt a special closeness to him since they shared the same age. She couldn't bring herself to go to that funeral.

And now there was Allen...

Karen lit another cigarette and quickly stuffed her hands in her jacket to block them from the persistent wind.

"Karen?"

She looked up from her shaking knees and saw Stacey Francis standing above her. Stacey was wrapped in layers of grey fabrics. Grey sweater, grey coat, grey scarf and pants. She wasn't a large lady, but she appeared to be so. She gained weight in a circular manner. She was on the verge of looking like a bouncy ball with bright, red cheeks. "Why are you sitting out in the cold, sweetie?"

Karen smiled. Stacey called everyone 'sweetie.' "It's really not that cold. I just wanted to smoke first before I went inside."

"Then why are your knees shaking?"

Karen glanced down at them, then mumbled around her cigarette, "It's the wind chill."

Stacey turned her gaze to the entrance of the church. She sighed and wrapped the scarf tighter around her neck. "Poor Allen. Did you know him very well?"

Karen shook her head and put the cigarette out on the steps. "Not really. I had seen him once or twice at the office. And when Larry had that party at his house...remember? When he invited the whole office just for the hell of it? I ran into him there. But that was it." She paused and stared at the thin plume of smoke coming up from the dying cigarette ashes. "I still can't really believe what happened."

"Oh I know. Poor thing! Did you hear about how many times he was *stabbed*?"

Karen winced and nodded.

"I mean, oh I'm sorry! There's no reason to talk about those things now. We just need to send him off right."

Karen nodded again and gave a thin smile.

"Come on, let's go in before we freeze." Stacey held out both of her hands, which were hidden inside grey gloves.

Karen glanced at them, then toward Stacey's rosy cheeks. "I'll be in there in a minute." She didn't even attempt to test her knees this time.

"You sure you're okay?"

"Yeah," she replied and tried her best to give a warm smile. Stacey began walking up the steps past her. "It's just that..."

Stacey turned back toward her. "What was that, sweetie?"

Karen shook her head and waved her on to go ahead. After she left, Karen looked at the trees that surrounded the church. Their leaves were dried out and different shades of brown. The grass, still a vibrant green, was hidden behind the leaves that had broken off. Leaving the limbs sparse and naked.

"It's just that," she finished to herself, "it seems like everything around us is dying."

Janus

Please hear me, Janus
Time appears to be unaware
The world tilts toward imbalance
Sun and moon are married in the starry air
I go forward, following your wise glance
Ignorant of the equal and opposite one you wear

"When will I learn to shut up?" Allen Carter asked himself as he walked through the streets of downtown Winsor. He had left the Slanted Donkey over an hour before. He turned a corner and came to a halt. He stared at the empty street, barren except for litter. His car wasn't there. Allen cursed, turned back and began going in the opposite direction. It was the third time he had lost his bearings.

"Maybe I should call Dylan," he mumbled, "maybe he's still at the bar." He took out his phone and began dialing. Then he shook his head and placed it back in his pocket. "No, I need to leave him alone. Probably doesn't even want to talk to me. Why can't I keep my mouth shut?" he asked ironically.

He looked down one of the side streets. In the distance, he could see the tall silhouette of the public library touching the night sky. "Was I parked near the library?" He scrunched his brow and pushed the eyeglasses back up his nose. "Yes! Yes I was." He quickened his pace and sprinted down the street.

A few blocks down, he neared a couple heading in the opposite direction. He slowed to a walk and gave them a furtive glance. The man and woman were holding hands and smiling at each other. Allen looked away and stared at the sidewalk as he passed by them. He glanced back at them and saw the man wrap his arm around the woman's waist as she tilted her head into his shoulder. Allen watched them walk away from him, then he turned back and continued toward the library, stuffing his hands deeply into his pants pockets.

After he had gone down another block, he began to sprint again. "Almost there, almost there," he muttered between breaths. This section of downtown was occupied with office buildings and banks; there were no bars. That being the case, there were also no *people on the street but Allen, so he found himself talking out loud insistently. "Next time I do this, I'm parking right on the side of the bar. Don't care what I have to pay. This is ridiculous." He slowed to a brisk walk as he started having trouble catching his breath. He took off his glasses, wiped the lenses on his undershirt, then placed them back on to the bridge of his nose. With his index finger, he pushed the frame back to the preferred spot and---*

Someone was standing in the middle of the street. Facing him.

He was so startled, he tripped over his own feet. He was able to regain his balance before falling down. The man, at least he thought it was a man, was about twenty feet away from him. It was dressed in all black clothing, from head to toe. Black jacket, shirt, jeans, boots and gloves. Over its head was a mask so dark that it merged with the shadows, making any features or outlines almost impossible. The figure was still, excluding the small movements of its breathing.

"Jesus!" Allen exclaimed and forced a brief laugh, "You scared the hell out of me." He gave a smile and laughed again. The figure remained still. "Are you lost too?" he continued, "Took me a while to get my bearings. Happens every time." The figure remained still. "Um..." Allen hesitated, "Still dressed up for Halloween? I missed that a couple weeks back."

The figure remained still.

"This guy's a psycho," Allen muttered softly, "I'll just go past him." He began to walk forward on the sidewalk. After taking a couple of steps, the figure on the street moved. It took a few steps over to the side to reach the sidewalk and turned to face him again, now directly in front of him. Allen stopped and took a step back. "What the hell's your problem?!"

The figure was still again.

He stepped out into the street to walk over to the other sidewalk. The figure did the same. "Why are you---!" He stopped as he caught a flash of light out of the corner of his vision. He adjusted his glasses and glanced down. The figure was holding something shiny in its hand. He squinted at it, then his eyes widened and he took a couple steps back. The figure was holding a box cutter in its hand, blade fully extended. He took another step back and the figure took one toward him. "Wait," Allen held up his hands, "what do you---" The figure took another step, now only a few feet from him.

Allen turned around and began running as fast as he could. He started screaming. He wanted to call out for help, but couldn't form any words. He felt it as the figure gripped the collar of his jacket. Felt it as the figure swiped the blade across his back, cutting through the jacket, the shirt and the flesh underneath. He spun around and raised his arms up to defend himself. He felt it as the blade cut his arms and his face.

Allen continued to scream, but his screams were quickly silenced. And never returned.

My City

    My city doesn't care about relationships. In Gerald Park, summer of '88, on top of the merry-go-round, Jack Lynch asked Christina Field to be his girlfriend. She said yes. Beaming, he leapt off the merry-go-round and picked a flower. He twisted and knotted it until it became a crude simulacrum of an engagement ring. He slipped it loosely on her finger and asked her if she would be his forever. She said yes.

    Jack let out a cheer and ran around Christina, repeating her name. He couldn't wait to tell his friends out on the playground the next day. But on the next day, she told Jack that she just wanted to stay as his friend. There was too much pressure from her classmates; *every*one was talking about them.

    Jack was crushed. He walked away without a word. During class, he stared at the back of her head, trying to decipher her thoughts. The more he tried, the angrier he became. He finally resorted to writing her an ugly, nasty note that he hoped would cause her pain. Like the pain he felt. He passed the note around the class until it reached her. He gripped the sides of his desk, anxiously waiting for the moment when she unfolded the note. The classroom was forgotten, the school was forgotten. All that mattered was seeing her hunch over her desk, reading the note. He watched as her shoulders sagged and her face reddened.

    And the city remained the same.

    *   *   *   *   *   *   *   *   *   *

    My city doesn't care about world events. Bryan Doyle was in a metal workshop, attempting to finish the project that had been assigned earlier that week. The goal was to create a three dimensional metal sculpture based off of an abstract, two dimensional drawing. The concept itself was so abstract to him that Bryan kept hitting a wall, metaphorically, and having to start over from scratch.

He stepped back, scrutinized the hunk of metal in front of him and was about to pick it up to toss it in the trash when he noticed that the music had stopped. The radio was mostly used for background noise since it could barely be heard over the sounds of the torches and saws. Yet whenever someone decided to take a break and let their minds work out some puzzle that stumped them, they would lean back and absorb the music tunes for a few minutes.

Bryan turned toward the corner office where the radio was kept and saw five people huddled around it. He took off his work goggles and walked over to the office. As he got closer, he could hear that a news report was being played. He tried to pick up what was being said, but couldn't get a grasp on the situation. The newscaster had a note of panic in her voice and kept halting in the report.

"What's going on?"

Two of the people around the radio shushed him and motioned for him to be quiet. Bryan shrugged and began to walk back to his table when the group let out a collective gasp. "Again?" one asked. "How could that happen with another one?" asked their neighbor.

"Will someone please say what the hell is going on?" Bryan asked impatiently.

A woman in the group turned toward him and she looked on the verge of tears. "A second plane just crashed into the Trade Center." She glanced back at the radio, "They thought the first one could have been a mistake. Like, maybe the pilot fell asleep or something. But now...a *second* one..." She shook her head and turned back around.

Bryan stared at their backs for a moment, then he tossed off his gloves and apron and walked outside. He went over to the guardrail that circled the second floor smoking area and peered over the ledge. No one was out smoking. Everyone he saw was either talking on a cellphone or walking briskly toward their vehicles.

"What does it mean?"

Bryan looked back over his shoulder at the voice. One of the men that was in the shop with him had also come outside. He was looking towards Bryan, but his eyes seemed unfocused and slightly glazed. "What did all that mean?" he asked.

Bryan exhaled slowly and went back to watching the people running across the grass. "It means," he responded, "that we're going to war."

And the city remained the same.

*　　*　　*　　*　　*　　*　　*　　*　　*　　*

My city doesn't care about Allen Carter.

Allen's body was found in the early morning following his attack. The sun still had not risen over the horizon. He had been stabbed and slashed so many times that his remains looked less like a body and more like a shredded slab of meat. The body sat in the middle of a huge pool of blood. The first officer on the scene merely stopped and stared at the pool for several moments before calling the incident in. There was so *much* of it.

Several people had heard Allen's screams, but none of them called the police. Each one believed someone else was already doing such and decided to not be involved. The person that did notify the police was someone who had also parked near the public library and had stumbled upon Allen's body on the way.

There were no witnesses to the attack; only one person claimed to have seen anything. An elderly man named Carl Pearson that worked on the cleaning crew for Hope Bank, about two blocks from the crime scene. Carl claimed that he had heard something outside the building, but didn't hear it clearly over the vacuum cleaner. He turned off the vacuum and stood by the glass entrance doors, peering out. He saw no movement and didn't hear the sounds again. He was almost certain he had heard a scream, but by who or what he just wasn't able to determine. He became more unsettled the longer the silence went on. He pressed his face against the glass and squinted into the darkness.

"And?" the policeman asked, "What did you see, sir?"

"A shadow," Carl replied, "standing right across the street from me. Staring at me." He shuddered and rubbed his arms.

"A...shadow?"

He nodded his head vigorously, "Yes. It was all black. Just standing there. I had to look back at it twice 'cause I couldn't tell if my eyes were playing tricks on me. But it was there. And as soon as I realized it, it took off. Down that street right over there. And as soon as I could bring myself to move again, I picked up that phone and called you."

The officer made notes on his pad. "Anything about the clothing that you could describe? Was this person big? Small?"

Carl shook his head. "There was nothing to *see*, don't you understand? It was just a *shape*."

The following day, the local news reported that Allen Carter had been murdered and that there were currently no leads. The police chief was quoted as saying that they were looking into all possibilities, including the chance that the attack might be linked to others that had happened around the city. He pleaded for the public to come forward with any information that could help bring the killer to justice.

And the city stayed the same.

Red Downpour

"Do you see what I see? What I've come to see?"
"I see the sky raining blood."

  Thankfully, the man found himself to be calm once again. It always made him calm.
  He stood on the street corner allowing the rain to wash over him and roll down his coat sleeves. He tilted his head toward the sky and let the droplets beat softly, rhythmically against his closed eye lids. He felt the slight shifts in the air as a pedestrian came within arm's length.
  The falling rain that was lightly rolling down his scalp felt like an old lover that enjoyed combing his hair with its fingertips. The blaring horn from a speeding car shook him from his daydream and he opened his eyes. The glaring headlights were blinding and disorienting.
  Then the man remembered where he was.
  He looked over his shoulder back at the hotel. On the fifth floor, third from the right, the lamps were still burning brightly. It still appeared as if someone lived there.
  He turned around and began his slow, steady pace down the sidewalk. The rain continued its persistent drumming upon his person, yet he barely noticed it anymore; he was searching for something specific. When he spotted it, he glanced both ways, and then sprinted across the street. As he reached the other side, he tossed two leather gloves into the half-filled wastebasket. He continued his way past and didn't glance back.
  Any passerby who happened to look in the wastebasket merely saw two gloves, soaked from the downpour.
  Not even when the streetlight above flickered to life did anyone notice all the red stains and streaks that covered them.

__Fireflies, pt. 1__

Everyone can see that there's nothing to see
And have nothing to say about living in the world today
It's been taken to heart that the present's been ripped apart
Everything's being saved and shipped through the airwaves
Forward steps have no guide and pull more to the side
And all are without sight when there's no longer a light

CLICK

---And that was 'I Didn't Come Here To Party' by The Bangers. Off of their new album *Banged Up*. It's the second single and, I must admit, I didn't really care for the last one. Did you, Susie?

---Well, David, I wouldn't say I *loved* it, but it was enjoyable, you know. It wasn't a song that I regretted we were playing.

---And I wouldn't say that either. I just meant that they haven't really had a huge hit on the radio since, uh, what was it?...help me out here.

---'One Thousand Ways To Die'?

---That's the one! I didn't agree with what the song was about, or whatever, but it was really catchy. I didn't feel like their recent songs have done that.

---All bands eventually reach their peak, so to speak. Maybe they've passed it?

---Could be. Anyway, now is about the time in the program where we usually talk about the weather forecasts and community events for the weekend, but I would prefer, if our listeners wouldn't mind, to talk about…well, the murders---

---Oh lord…

---that have been happening. Around the city.

---It's horrible. Just horrible. To think that could happen in this city…

---And that's one of the points that I would like to make. You grow up somewhere---let's say Winsor is your hometown, like me---and you read about the horrible things happening in New York or Baltimore or wherever. And you---at least *I do*---think to yourself, "I'm glad that kind of thing doesn't happen here." Or, "That would *never* happen in my town."

---That's exactly right, David. I mean, we've *never*…at least not in my lifetime, had something like this. You know? Or am I missing something?

---No, no, you're not wrong, but I also think we should probably accept the fact that a lot of things---good things, bad things, what have you---just go under the radar. I mean, right now, right this minute, there's probably something really terrible that's happening. Maybe even in our city. That won't make the news. That will be ignored and everyone can pretend like things are just fine.

---Things *were* just fine until recently. Now I'm scared to go *any*where at night. At least by myself.

---But that's the real point I wanted to get to, Susie, and then I will return back to the program. I apologize to any of our listeners that are, I don't know, aggravated or whatever that we're talking about this, but I feel it's important to talk about these things and not ignore them.

---I agree, I agree.

---But the point I wanted to make was that these things *have* been happening. There have been murders, assaults, stabbings, all that. And we just look the other way. So that we can remain comfortable, so we can go out at night, so we can tell ourselves that there's nothing wrong. And go about our day…anyway, that's all I wanted to say about that. Sorry for getting off topic here, folks. Up next we have a song that's been pretty popular with our listeners. It's the new one by---

CLICK

* * * * * * * * * *

I remember a time when Winsor was a much smaller town.

I know that sounds clichéd, and I feel like one for stating it, but it's amazing to reflect on a city's landscape twenty, thirty years prior and compare it to present day. Before the highway extensions and the unnecessary shopping centers, there was a large wooded area that covered the north side of Winsor. I would, as a child, go walking through it every day. Which in hindsight was a pretty dangerous thing for a child to do considering how it was bursting with wildlife.

I would always see snakes and banana spiders and rabbits and raccoons. Oh my! We had even captured a rabbit once and tried to keep him as a pet. I use the term 'tried' because the entire incident ended tragically and quite quickly. I won't go into details, but it involved our housecat that showed herself for having a very large appetite.

At night, the woods would light up with dozens and dozens, or maybe hundreds, of fireflies. I hated the night and the darkness that came with it, but I loved to go out and watch the fireflies. The living, swirling light bulbs filled me with wonder, as I'm sure it did most children. Is that another cliché? I apologize. I would then try to capture that wonder in my hands; to hold the light and feel the small body buzz around in my palms.

Which would kill them, of course. Then the sadness would come. Short lived though, because there were so many of them flying through the air. The death of one meant so little.

Then all of the fireflies died, of course. So did the snakes and rabbits and raccoons. The spiders persevered to an extent, the sneaky bastards. It began with the expansion of Interstate 50. The city had remained the same for a while, and there were those that wanted change. So how do you go about facilitating that? By tourism and migration. So Interstate 50, which was little more than a service road for a very long time, became a major interstate and the main travel route for traffic going through and coming into Winsor.

And it brought along a wall of sound. The trees (oh, so many trees!) had acted like natural sound sponges, soaking up all the excess noise and leaving not much more than the sounds of crickets and swaying branches. But in order to have the expanded roads and swelled populations, the trees have to go. Of course.

Without them, Winsor suddenly became a city full of the busy cacophony of motor vehicles and motorways. Where there once appeared to be citywide docility, now seemed to be endless activity. There was one small batch of the large wooden area that was left behind, cornered off to the side of Grey Park. After I had started college, and during a moment of painfully strong nostalgia, I decided to walk through the woods one time after a visit to my parents' house. I walked around the trees and couldn't even hear the sound of my shoes crunching the leaves and branches underfoot; all I heard were passing cars.

The entire area also appeared lifeless. It seemed that not even the majority of the spiders could live in this pathetic environment. It was now just a dying husk slowly being picked away next to a strip mall.

That's when I finally felt a sense of old age, though that may be a strange thing for someone to say that's currently in their mid-thirties. As I was growing up, I never had a sense of my age. I just felt…like myself. I would overhear so many people say, "Oh, I wish I was such and such age again," or "If I could go back ten years…" And so on. I would always think, "Why? What difference would ten or twenty years make? I still felt like myself back then, more or less." But standing in the near-lifeless strip of trees, and remembering the animals that used to thrive but were now dead and gone, I felt really old. It was like I was continuing to live my life, changing very little outside of cosmetically speaking, yet the world around me was becoming more industrialized and mechanical. Which is a strange way to feel considering that I was born into an already heavily-mechanical world. Somehow, we've gone even further with our love affair with machinery and digital imagery.

I felt like a relic buried and forgotten until, one day, I awakened to realize that someone had placed me in the middle of the discount aisle at a brightly, artificially lit supermarket. Does the world even need animals anymore? The more robotic and digitized the world becomes, the less it looks like we give a damn about living, breathing organisms.

I don't know where I'm going with this. I let my mind wander too much on my drives to work. Maybe everything is just like the radio DJ said: Things have always been this way, people just take too long to notice and react accordingly. Yet I can't help, as I go through my city on my morning drives, to feel like something is really different. Something is *fundamentally* wrong with our times. I can feel a darkness creeping inside, one that used to be kept out by the trees and rabbits and snakes and even the sneaky spiders. One that's covering everything and everyone.

And there are no more fireflies to push it back.

*   *   *   *   *   *   *   *   *   *

Ah, Ballet Films. Stupid name, right? It was supposed to reflect our ability to deftly cover several different genres. 'Dance' from one to the other and so on. But if one would look at the studio's filmography (not that many would care to do so), they would not see a balancing act of genre-hopping. They would just see horror movies.

And that would be accurate because it's all that we do. The studio has only been around for five years and we learned very quickly that people don't care about local, independent dramas and comedies. But horror films? They eat that up like zombies. For camp or pure entertainment value, they reel 'em in.

So now we are a locally owned and operated film studio, producing exclusively horror movies with a name that didn't seem to make any sense. So it goes. I get to criticize it all, and I do daily, since I work there. My official title is Screenwriter and that's what you'll see in the credits, but a more accurate one would be Studio Bitch. We don't write anything that we want; we're given projects. And we can't approach those projects in any manner that we please. The studio lays down guidelines for the scripts and deadlines to be met. Hell, they start production on some of the things before we're even done writing it all out. Sometimes, we have to write scenes to *match* the finished set pieces.

It's all kind of backwards, at least I think so. And…what's this? A new text from the director, starting with the word "URGENT." Oh this is can't be good. Let's see what it says…another scene that she's not going to be in? Seriously? How is she even still the lead in this film? And what version are we on now? Pink or is it yellow? I think we were on version pink last week but, by god, we'll run out of colors before we're finished shooting. There's no logic behind the color system at all. We should just number the scripts. Version 1, 2, 100. Or maybe they don't want the crew paying attention to how half-assed this all is. Or maybe---

"Talking to yourself again, Dylan?"

I smile and look up from my phone. She caught me again. "Karen Young," I reply, "as I live and breathe. Would you believe me if I said otherwise?"

Fireflies, pt. 2

      Holy mother of god, I hate this god damned Bullpen. Everyone's desks are cramped and overstuffed because they're sitting right on freaking top of each other. Everything on my desk, *every*thing, is either on top of something else or right next to me. Pens are always rolling across my desk and spilling on to the floor. The second I pick them up, something else spills over. Ohmygod I hate it here. When things weren't so crazy stupid obnoxiously busy, it was okay here I guess. I still didn't *love* it but it was better. Who loves their job anyway?? A psycho, that's who. But then we got asked by the Fantasy Channel to work on one of their scripts. Which we did. But I guess we did it too well. Our last two movies were for them, now we have two *more* that we're doing. And all of it is that stupid lame horror shit. I thought we did other things? Isn't that what our commercial says? But now we got money hungry and the studio was like, "oh, Fantasy? Why yes, sir, master sir! Anything for you, master sir!" So they hired more people because they expected a lot more business. Hired *before* we got the business. Isn't that dumb?? We're in a building that was built for a work environment of, what, seventy? Eighty people? Now we have one hundred and three. And employees sitting on top of each other, trying to work. Shuffled and packed like cattle. That's why we call it The Bullpen. Do you see why I'm aggravated? Every day, my elbows are bumping and---that's it. That one goes into the trash! From now on, everything that falls on the floor is going right in the can. I don't have time to spend 99% of my day picking crap up. I put my head in my hands and sigh. Loudly. I can hear what everyone is saying around me. The entire office. I can always hear them. I look for my headphones, so I could plug them into my phone. The remaining 1 or whatever percent of my day that doesn't go to picking shit up, goes to music. I'm just a hardcore worker like that. I reach under the pile where my headphones should have been. Not there. Damn it. Where'd they go now? My hands continue to dig and shuffle through the piles blindly. Where the hell where they? Behind me, I can hear John and Haley talking. Not like I was *listening* to them. Or trying to. It couldn't be helped.

"Do you know if Princess Ramada showed up for work today?"

"I think she's here, but I don't think she's working."

"What else is new? Why did they hire her anyway?"

"Well, she's like a mini-celebrity or something. If that exists. You know, like with T.V. movies and such."

"So if I watched a lot of T.V., I'd be impressed with her presence?"

"Not saying that…just saying you'd recognize her."

"She must have rich parents or something because she's missed most of the shooting days that she was supposed to be a part of."

"I don't know about that, but her *name* is the only reason people are gonna watch this lame-ass show."

"If we ever finish it. I mean, seriously? I hear we're supposed to get another script today. How are you supposed to plan anything out like that?"

"It's always been ass-backwards here. It's just worse now cause we got more shit to do."

I still can't find my headphones. So I get up and walk around. I pass by the breakroom and restrooms. Going nowhere specific. I just needed to move around, to feel like I was out of my cage. I need to feel that briefly each day before I go back to feeling like cattle.

* * * * * * * * * *

Someone let the coffee burn again. Sonofabitch. I smell the pot again, seriously considering pouring myself a cup. I want coffee that badly. I sigh and put the pot down again. Some intern will probably finish it off. I begin walking back to my cramped cluttered cubicle. I can see the pile of junk from here and can tell already that at least one or two things made it back to the floor. Holy cow, it's hard to breathe in here. I clutch at my chest and try to rub away the tightness that's formed there. Is this it? Am I finally being smothered to death by The Bullpen? I quickly spin around and start walking toward the smoking area. God I needed some fresh air. Passing through the central hallway, I realize that my jacket is still hanging on the back of my chair. At my desk. Sonofabitch. Do I just suck it up and deal with the cold while I smoke? *I can't* go back. Not yet. I would die. Right in the middle of this---Oh, hello. I believe I know this gentleman. He's looking down at his cellphone, so he hasn't noticed me yet. He also appears to be wearing at least two shirts underneath a hoodie. I shake my head. Isn't it almost 80 degrees in here? It's not like he's outside. I walk over to him and see that his lips are forming words that I can't hear. "Talking to yourself again, Dylan?" I ask him.

Dylan smiles and glances up from his phone. "Karen Young, as I live and breathe. Would you believe me if I said otherwise?"

"I'm sorry, did we just meet?"

He laughs, "Alright, no point in trying this time. Lesson learned." He looks back down on his phone.

"What's that?" I ask while pointing at the screen, "Are you trying to be rude or is that important?"

He lets out a short huff and gives me a sidelong glance. "If you really must know, it's---oh hell. Just read it yourself. Probably quicker that way."

He hands the phone to me and I start reading the text that he has open. "Are they serious?" I ask after a minute, "Another script version?"

He takes the phone back and puts it in his pocket, "Oh, they're serious alright. I wish it was some sort of overly elaborate practical joke, but alas, I don't think they have a sense of humor." He clutches at his chest and turns his head toward the ceiling, eyes closed. "If they keep this up, I will literally *die*."

I lower my eyelids and stare into his smug mug. "You joshin' me?"

He opens his eyes and smiles again. "Maybe just a little…but seriously, they are killing me with all this crap."

"Well, what's their excuse this time? And what color are we on anyway? Yellow?"

"I think it's pink," he mumbles, "but then again, who knows? We've gone through more scripts than I do socks." He lifts his hand and starts scratching at his hairline. Oh my god he does this all the freaking time. He's handsome, but there was no doubt that he was going to be bald one day. Not with that receding hairline. And him scratching the hell out of it *can't* be helping. One day, his fingers are going to come away bloody, I swear.

I smack his hand away and come really close to flat-out slapping his face. "Would you *stop* that? What's the matter with you?"

"Sorry, sorry. You know it's a habit. And talking about script versions makes my skin crawl."

"So what's the reason for this one? Or is it the same one as always?"

He throws his hands up. "The same freaking reason. What else? They hired a freaking lead who can't even show up for any of the freaking shooting days! So we rearrange our schedules, rewrite the *scenes*, just to keep her in the freaking movie." He pauses and takes a breath, "Freaking bullshit."

I shake my head, "I don't even know how she gets work. She's dropped out of the last two movies she was cast for, then for the ones that she's *in*, she trash-talks them! Remember when that happened? What was that movie…"

"*Love Lives Eternal.*"

I snap my fingers, "Right! She called everyone on the set an idiot and said she was embarrassed to be the star. Ooooh, my blood boiled when I saw that. And I didn't even work on that one!"

He laughs, "I remember that. And the interviewer got so flustered, he just kept saying her name over and over. 'B-but, Alexis! But, Miss Ramada!'"

We both continue to laugh. It feels good; can't remember laughing hard like that in a while. After it dies down, we stand in silence for a bit. Nothing else to really say, but not wanting to separate just yet. He then becomes very serious and looks off to the side. "Hey, um," he furrows his brow and continues to avoid looking at me, "have you been having nightmares?"

Where the heck is this coming from? "You mean like, ever?" I respond, trying to lighten his mood, "As in, have I ever had one and do I know what it is? Hmmm, don't think so."

He gives a thin, strained smile. Well, a part of one. "I usually never dream," he says, "It's very rare that I do. But for the past three weeks, I've had several of them. And they've all been nightmares."

Three weeks? Oh…since---"You mean since…Allen?"

He nods and begins to scratch his hairline again. I let him be. "Yeah. And they're all…*similar*. I mean, thematically."

"Explain."

"Well," he sighs and purses his lips, "I'll just describe the last one to you. So, I'm walking on the streets in between a group of buildings so tall that I can't see the tops of them. Or even the sky, for that matter. And under my feet are piles and piles of leaves. Dead leaves, brown and crunching with every step. And standing in front of the buildings are shadows. Hundreds of them. And they're all staring at me."

"The shadows were staring?"

"Yeah, it…it was like they were standing around, like regular people. I couldn't see their eyes, but I knew that they were watching everything I did. I tried to run, but my legs were being held down by all the leaves. The harder I tried, the more they held my feet down…then I woke up."

"Geez," I say, having nothing else to give, "are they all like that?"

"Not exactly. They all have the same shadowy figures and such, and I'm trying to get away. And I never can." He pauses, then looks at me intently, "So have you? Had them as well?"

I try to look out of a nearby window, so that I can see the bare trees and the cold ground still covered with leaves, but I forgot we are still in the middle of this damn stupid crazy-ass building. I look toward the wall anyway, as if a window *was* there. "I haven't had nightmares, no, but something else has been bugging me since the funeral."

"Such as?"

"…I don't know. I really don't. It's as if something is just *off*, you know? Like, I can't put my finger on it, but every time I can finally get away from that damn desk, this *office*, and I'm driving around outside, I can feel…like something's missing or changed." He nods his head. Does he want me to shut up? Or does he know what I'm trying to say? Do I even know myself? "Something is just *wrong*, like really wrong in Winsor. And I don't know what it is or why I feel this way. But I *need* it to go away."

Time and Time Again

Going down this road
Less the desire to turn back
Reckless and immature
Acute observations of the facts
There needs to be a change
An escape from the sin
Run in the circles we've paved
Time and time again

    Louis Connelly lifted the beer can to his mouth and finished off the remainder of the drink. Another one down; the tally was up to eight.

    Louis believed that if he drank enough, reached a state of complete insobriety, then he wouldn't have to deal with the rest of the evening. He didn't even care about how bad off he would be in the morning.

    The past few months had been rocky between him and his wife Jamie. When it started, he had noticed that she was less communicative than usual. It eventually reached a point where she was talking only just as much as him in the conversations. In other words, barely at all. He questioned this and she responded that it was "nothing. Don't worry about it."

    This was usually the response he received when he had done something to upset and/or anger her. But within a few hours, she generally would explain to him what the offense was. Considering that didn't take place, he continued to wait for her to speak up about it.

    It didn't happen, and the tension between them worsened. He finally confronted her about it and she stated that she had been having issues with her parents; asked for him to not worry about it. He agreed to, but mentioned that he would appreciate it if she filled him in on these situations. "You always want me to talk with you about these things," he told her, "but you aren't doing the same." A look of surprise filled her features and Louis felt a strange satisfaction, as if he had won some sort of contest. Jamie promised to work harder in the future and apologized.

Then it continued to spiral downward.

A few days ago, his wife came to him with the suggestion that they separate for a while. A severe tightening of the muscles of his chest labored his breathing and his mind became sluggish. He didn't know how to respond to something like that. For a long time, he stood in stunned silence while his mind tried to make sense of the situation.

Then words poured out of him. He demanded explanations; he alternated between apologizing for unknown offenses and cursing her very being. He left his home in a rush and spent the entire night driving. At work the following morning, he was so tired and emotionally exhausted that it took everything for him to give the briefest responses. Unconsciously, he mirrored his wife by stating, "Nothing. Don't worry about it," to all the questions.

That night he returned home wanting nothing more than to head straight to the bedroom and make up all the sleep he had missed. But Jamie had other plans. She felt that the events of the previous night needed to be settled before going on any further. He tried to follow the discussion and answer as politely as possible, but the image of his bed wouldn't leave his mind. He quickly became irritable with her and started snapping back, just like the night before. She became distant and fell silent. Awkwardly, Louis mentioned about going to sleep and continuing the discussion the next day. Jamie said she would join him later and walked into the kitchen without another word.

She never came to bed, and in the morning she was gone.

Throughout the day, he had tried calling her by her cellphone and at the office. He had no luck with either one. When he came home from work, her car still wasn't in the driveway. He drove two streets over to Curtis Lane and stopped by Gwen Macey's home; a friend of his wife. She notified him that she didn't have a clue to Jamie's whereabouts either and asked him if he could please keep her updated on the situation. When Louis turned back on to Carpenter Lane, his phone began to ring. It was Jamie. She told him that she was going to stay with her sister for the time being; didn't feel that it was a good idea for them to be together currently. She would be by in the next couple days, at some point, to collect some things.

He made several attempts to apologize to her, but she proceeded to speak as if he had said nothing. When she had finished, she told him "goodbye" and hung up without waiting for his responses. Again, Louis found himself in stunned silence as he tried to understand the situation. In a daze, he parked his car at home, turned it off and started to walk through the neighborhood.

Letting his feet guide him and choosing to not think about it, he found himself at a nearby gas station. He had no idea how long he had been walking, but the sun had nearly set completely past the horizon. He walked into the station and wandered through the aisles, glancing over the consumables with disinterest. After a few minutes, the cashier asked if he needed any assistance. "Yes," Louis responded, "get me a case of beer. I don't give a shit about the brand, but get me the largest size you've got."

* * * * * * * * *

Louis was halfway through another beer when he became severely nauseated. The beer in his gut started heading back up his throat and he had to force it down. *Alright, I can take a hint,* he thought, *enough is enough.* Louis stood upright on the merry-go-round and glanced around Grey Park. The park was deserted. When he had first shown up, a few stray cars had been sitting in the parking lot. Now it appeared that he was the only person left.

He glanced down at the remaining beer cans, felt the bile rise again and began walking away from them with a hand to his mouth. *Maybe some kid'll find 'em. Hate for it all to go to waste.* He stumbled over his own feet. Corrected his balance and tried again. He was having a difficult time even walking in a semi-straight line. His vision was constantly bouncing around.

Where the hell's the bathroom? He could feel urine trying to push its way out of his body and he began to frantically look around the park. He spotted a lone, slim structure in the distance that appeared to have only one door. He began to head in that direction. The pressure began building up and he quickened the pace as much as possible. *Gonna fucking piss myself. Why the hell didn't I go earlier?* The distance between him and the building was quickly shortening. He started to wheeze slightly and had to reclaim his balance after tripping over a rock or branch a few times.

Then his knee exploded.

Louis cried out and fell straight down on to the ground. He split his forehead open on a rock, but didn't feel the pain since it was all concentrated on his kneecap. He moaned and looked over to his leg. The area of his jeans around his knee was shredded and soaked. He touched his hand to the spot and it came away covered in blood. "What's going on?!" he cried out, "What the hell is this?!"

He attempted to move his leg and pain shot through him like an electric shock. He suddenly loss half his vision and felt something running down the right half of his face. The cut in his forehead was bleeding severely. He placed his hands on his thigh and started to lift his leg up. Another wave of pain hit him and he let go of the leg and fell back against the ground with a cry. He was huffing from the exertion and it was a few moments before he realized there was something right outside his scope of vision.

He flicked his head over to the side and saw that a man was standing right next to him. Or what appeared to be a man. The figure was dressed in all dark colors that seemed to be solid black in the muted light. Louis struggled to speak, "Oh, oh god." Blood was pouring into his mouth and he had to spit it back out before he said more. "Please, pl-please help me, man. I think I, oh god I got fuckin' *shot!*" He raised his gaze to the figure's face and his mind struggled to understand what he was seeing. The face was all black and seamless; it mimicked the shapes and contours of features without having any defining characteristics. It appeared to be some sort of skintight mask, but it didn't appear to be made out of cloth or fabric. It looked more like flesh or rubber.

Louis didn't know how long he stared at the face with his one eye, but he eventually forced himself to lift his hand toward the figure. "Please help me up. I...I can't, I tried—" He stopped trying to explain himself and held his arm up for the person to take hold. The figure continued to stand still, with the head slightly turned down toward Louis.

His arm became heavy, so Louis let it drop and wiped some of the blood off his cheek. He began to lift the other one and stopped as he heard a light tapping sound and turned his eye toward it. The figure was repeatedly tapping something against its leg. Louis's brow furrowed and a new wave of pain spread through his head. He tried to process what he was looking at through the pain. When he did, his eye widened and a chill went through his body.

In the figure's gloved hand was a ruger 9mm handgun. It was held loosely, almost casually, as it was being tapped against the thigh. "D-did...did *you?*" Louis struggled to get his words out, "You-*you* fucking, you fucking *shot me?!*" The figure continued to stare at him, continued to tap the gun. "Who the hell *are* you? Why would you *do* this to me?!"

Tap, tap, tap, was the only response he received.

"Listen what do—money? You want my...? Is that it?"

Tap, tap, tap.

"Here, take my wallet, it's *yours*! I don't fuckin' want it!"

Tap, tap, tap.

Louis's heart felt like it was beating through his ribcage and about to leap from his chest. He felt the front of his jeans getting wet and spreading warmth across his hips. "Oh, oh please don't, I-I—" The figure continued to stare, to tap. Louis felt tears come to his eyes and his remaining vision became a blur. "Just let me go," he cried, "I'll never…I'll never say any—"

In a flash of movements, the figure stepped forward, raised the gun and fired it point blank into Louis's face. There was a brief pause as Louis's muffled, blood-choked cry spit out then four more shots emanated. One minute passed, then six more gunshots followed. And then there was silence.

The silence was broken shortly after as police sirens in the distance started and sharply increased in volume as the distance shortened. When the police officers arrived at the scene, they found the bloody remains of Louis Connelly rendered unrecognizable from the attack.

There was no one with him and no sign that anyone ever was.

The Figure, pt. 1

The man was calm again. It always made him calm...

Dylan opened his eyes and knew immediately that something was wrong.

He lifted his head slightly from the pillow and peered around the bedroom. His eyes, though adjusted to the darkness, had difficulty making out any defined shapes. Everything appeared to be merely a series of shadows.

He propped himself up on his elbows and looked over the sides of his bed. Nothing. He tilted his head to the side and strained to pick up any unusual noises. Nothing. His eyes scanned the bedroom once more. Nothing by the closet, nothing by the dresser, nothing by the door, nothing by the bath---

To the left of his bed, there was a shadow, darker than the rest, standing in the middle of the floor. He squinted at it. He couldn't make out its shape; define the edges. There was just a deep blackness that seemed to swallow the weak rays of light that seeped through the window.

He squinted harder at the shadow. In a panic, he realized that the shape had gotten closer to him. It was now merely a foot away from the edge of the bed. Dylan opened his mouth to yell out. The shadow raised a bright, sharp object. Before he could see what it was, the shadow brought the object down with great force and stabbed him in-between the lungs.

* * * * * * * * *

Dylan opened his eyes and looked over at the clock. 2:33 a.m. He placed his hand on his chest and rubbed the spot where he had been stabbed. It still hurt. With every breath, he felt the pain down to his spine.

He looked around the bedroom, mimicking his dream. *I'm awake now. Calm down.* His heart was beating rapidly and every pulse aggravated the phantom wound. He went to sit upright and found his body unresponsive. He looked down at his legs and willed them to move. They remained stubbornly immobile. *I'm awake now. I'm awake. So why can't I move?* Dylan grunted and felt drops of sweat form on his forehead.

Something in the room laughed.

He stopped breathing and shifted his gaze upward. Standing above him was a dark figure, a shape. The void seemed to negate the air in the room and he found that he couldn't breathe anymore. The shape swept over him and enveloped his head in its arms. It laughed again; a slow, guttural sound that was more like a growl. *This isn't happening. This isn't real. Wake up, wake up, wake up.* The shape began tightening its grip and Dylan felt the bones in his skull crack and break under the pressure.

Wake up wake up wake up wake up wake up wake up wake up wake up.

The shape continued to laugh.

*   *   *   *   *   *   *   *   *

Dylan opened his eyes and woke up.

He immediately turned on the lamp sitting atop of the nightstand next to his bed. He surveyed the room slowly for any shadows. His heart was pounding quickly and each beat initiated phantom pains from his chest and head. He sighed and lightly scratched his hairline. The nightmares were becoming more frequent. The first one happened on the night following Allen's murder. It repeated itself at least twice a week for the past four consecutive weeks. And now there was Louis...

Dylan tossed his covers to the side and walked out into the hallway. On the way to the kitchen, he turned on every light switch that he came upon. Grabbed a drinking glass off the kitchen counter and filled it with tap water. He drank the water quickly; his mouth was dry and his throat was sore. Louis's body had been found at the beginning of the week. Or what remained of him. It had been difficult for the coroners to corroborate the dental records they received since most of Louis's skull had been obliterated from repeated gunshots.

Dylan gagged and spit out the remaining water. *Stop it, stop thinking about it.* He stepped back from the sink; his imagination was causing his sense of smell to pick up something similar to sewage. He went over to the living room window and opened it wide. Took a deep breath of the outside air. The phantom pains in his body persisted. He scratched his hairline again and looked down at the ground outside. It was covered with dead leaves, wet from the morning dew.

He sniffed the air again. Grimacing, he pulled his head back inside and shut the window. The air outside smelled of nothing but rot and decay.

Disconnect

"...And standing in front of the buildings are shadows. Hundreds of them. And they're all staring at me."
----Dylan Haddon

CLICK

Here is a crime procedural. A man reports the theft of his family's fortune. He meets up with the specialized detectives that solve these sorts of things every week. They question family, friends and co-workers, eventually getting closer and closer to the source. It comes back to the man, the one that originally reported the crime. Turns out he stole from his own family and covered it up because---*CLICK*

Here is a reality show. A group of strangers are forced to live in the same house together for six months. They argue constantly. No one can seem to reach a common viewpoint, not even between the romantic interests that form. These cause more arguments, actually, because the men and women that got together were also involved, in some way, with others in the group at the same---*CLICK*

Here is a sitcom comedy. A group of friends meet up daily to interact and go on some adventure or stop, what they consider, a crisis. Most events happen during the day, though all of the characters hold full-time jobs. Scenes at the workplace are not shown. Instead, the viewers get---

CLICK

Catherine-Lynn Bobbett continued to change the channel of the T.V. in front of her, generally every ten minutes or so. She never looked at the remote control or the T.V. while she did it. The set was merely on out of habit. And for the noise. It was too quiet in her apartment without it on.

In front of her was her laptop, sitting open on her coffee table. The open webpages were Facebook, Twitter, Instagram, Fox News and Myspace. Myspace was open simply to stream music. In her lap was her cellphone. Her attention was divided equally among social media sites, objective news and text messages. And like clockwork, she would raise her left hand (the one not being used socially) and change the T.V. channel.

The figure watched her silently. It stood behind her, off to her right. It was no more than ten feet away. If she looked over her shoulder, she would see it within an instant. Instead, she continued to give her full attention to the lifeless screens. The figure watched her as she watched her social life.

After it cut her throat, the screens watched her bleed out and wither like a dried husk. And their light was reflected in her lifeless eyes.

Me and My Gun

---The following is an excerpt from a witness report by detective Doug Ressler, on the murder of Louis Connelly:

When Laurie Francis responded, her voice was very light and I had to lean forward to hear her. "I kept checking out my window," she said, "waiting for the police to show up. At one point, I thought I saw something out of the corner of my eye. Like a dark shape. I thought it was just a reflection from my drapes or something. But when I moved them back, the shape didn't move." She bit her lip, "I stared at it for a moment, trying to figure out what it was. It was like my eyes were playing tricks on me. I couldn't tell if anything was really there and there wasn't enough light to tell otherwise. Then there was a flash of light, like maybe lightning or something, and for a brief moment I could see outside clearly. And there was no doubt in my mind that there was someone standing there across the street. Watching my home."

"Who was it, Mrs. Francis? Did you recognize this person?"

She shook her heard angrily. "I couldn't tell. As soon as I realized what was happening, I jumped back from the window. I pushed aside the curtains shortly after to see if they were still there, but they were gone. Just a clear patch of grass under that tree right out there. When the police were going around talking to my neighbors the next day, I told them what I'd seen, but I probably sounded hysterical." She gave a brief, humorless laugh, "I sound hysterical to myself. Even now. Hard to sound any other way if all I have to say is that I was terrified of a shadow."

Home Security, Firearms & Ammo Supply, was located on the corner of Washington and Carson. The building showed signs of considerable wear: peeling paint, an old window boarded up from the year prior, and one of the two opening doors was locked into place.

The man standing across the street continued to contemplate the building. One hand was casually scratching his short beard while the other hung limply. A couple walked out of the store. They were carrying a case and had their head bent over a sheet of paper, probably a receipt. The man watched them slowly walk away, and then he crossed the street and entered the store.

The inside of the store was surprisingly small. It only took a few steps from the doorway before he reached the front counter. Behind the counter was an open door with stacks of boxes. *Must be where they keep the inventory*, the man thought. He looked down at the glass countertop. Under it were a neatly arranged collection of handguns going from smallest size to largest, left to right. Next to each gun was a box of ammunition. Along the walls of the store were rifles and shotguns. Less thought seemed to have gone into their arrangement; merely rifles on one wall, shotguns on the other. It was dimly lit inside the store. Maybe intentionally so. In order to get a view of any of the weapons, the man had to lean right over them.

"Can I help you with something, pal?"

The man stood up straight and took in the store attendant. The attendant was wearing a faded, button-up blue jean shirt with no undershirt. The shirt had the name 'Jimmy' engraved on the left breast pocket. The man smiled; he couldn't remember the last time he saw someone's name on their shirt. The attendant's pants and shirt were both dirty and gave him the look of a mechanic that just came out from under a car. Under the dark red hair were brown eyes, framed by what seemed to be a permanent frown. "I'm not sure," the man responded, "just browsing. I guess."

Jimmy grunted and swept his arm over the glass counter. "Well, we got a large variety. As you can see. And don't think that I only have one or two of each gun." He pointed back over his shoulder, "If you need multiples, the storeroom's packed. In fact, most of this store is taken up by that back room."

"Yeah, I was wondering about that," the man replied and looked back toward the front doors, "When I saw this place from the street, it looked pretty large. Was kinda confused why it seemed so cramped in here."

Jimmy grunted again. "I hear you. I used to have a problem

with it. Was gonna do something else with the space; seemed like a waste having so much of it. But now I'm *glad* I have all this room in the back. Really glad. If I didn't, there's no way I could keep up with demand."

"Have you been seeing a lot more business lately?"

"*Have* I?" Jimmy let out a quick laugh that was quite similar to his grunts, "Brother, you know what my average sales were before now? I was doing 18, 19, 20 guns a week. Give or take. Know where I'm at now? *Over a hundred in the past week*!"

The man's eyes widened and he gave a low whistle. "Wow, that's quite a jump. Until you hear numbers like that, you forget about just how many people live in this city." He scrunched his brow. "I'm assuming it's all because of...well. The murders?"

"What else would it be?" Jimmy flicked his head toward the entrance, "Every one of them comes in here and feels the need to give me their life story about why they're buying the gun; how they plan to protect themselves. I couldn't give a shit, if you want me to be honest. As long as they pass the background check, the hell do I care? Just buy the gun, shut up and get out." He squinted at the street. "You been to Piercing Fire lately? Over by Colleen and Young street?"

"Oh! You mean the firing range. No, no, haven't been."

"Brother, I went by there last week and you would've sworn I walked into Walmart. Packs and packs of people as far as you could see. All there to try out their shiny, new, dangerous firearms. Look here, man, I turned around and walked right out. Don't have time to mess around with all that. You read me?"

The man gave a slight smile. "Do you believe all of the stuff that they're saying? Like on the news and such?"

"I don't know what you mean. You asking if I think people are getting *killed*?"

"No, no, no," the man bit his cheek and tried again, "What I meant was...it just seems like, oh I don't know. Unreal? Like, you hear people telling stories on the street or in a grocery or wherever.

And they talk about either seeing the killer or knowing someone that has. And they always describe him--or her--as being like a shadow or a shade. Something similar to that. The media does the same thing, though they've tried to spice it up lately as if there's a conspiracy going on." The man cleared his throat and took on a different affectation. " 'How could the police not have a suspect yet? This is a small town; where's the killer going to hide? Why isn't anyone trying to do something about this?' "

Jimmy gave another grunt/laugh. "Yeah, I heard some of that stuff. Look here, man, in one ear, out the other, you know? I say, you wanna do something? Then *do* something. Go get a gun and find the guy if you think you can do better than the cops. You read me? Find him and shoot him. 'Cause wherever he is, whether he's still in Winsor or he fled. Wherever he is, he's just a man. Ain't no shadow or shit like that. And a man can be shot and be killed. End of story."

The man smiled fully and nodded. "I agree with you completely, Jimmy. One hundred percent." He glanced back down at the glass counter. "I think I'll have to come back another time. Figure out what I want first. I don't want to take any more of your time." Then the man lowered his head a bit, almost in a bow, "Thank you very much, I appreciate all the help." He gave a brief wave and walked out of the store. He went back across the street and stood again on the street corner. On the side of the store, three women were grouped together having a conversation. One of them shot a quick look at the store, then back at the other women. Eventually, all three walked around the side and went into the building in a single file.

The man continued to look after them until the door had swung shut, then he turned and began to walk down the sidewalk away from Home Security, Firearms & Ammo Supply. He wondered, briefly, about the people he saw today. The ones walking out with cases and receipts and a renewed sense of confidence.

Would any of them really be able to use their shiny, new, dangerous firearms against him when it eventually became time to do so?

Investigative Reports

----The following is an excerpt from a witness report by detective Doug Ressler, on the murder of Allen Carter:

One person that heard the scream was Stanley Victor. He was lying on his bed, finishing up a marathon of all the sitcom episodes he had missed that week, when the scream pierced his bedroom. He reached for the remote control and muted the television. What the hell was that? *He waited, but the sound didn't repeat itself. He wasn't sure if it was his imagination, but the scream sounded like it got cut off abruptly.* Probably just some idiots foolin' around or something, *he told himself,* It doesn't concern you. *Stanley picked up the remote again and unmuted the T.V. The rest of his night played out the same way it had started; only now he periodically found himself pausing to listen to the night, to hear if the scream repeated itself.*
He couldn't explain why he was so disturbed by the fact that it never did.

Allen Carter wasn't the first. But who was?

Doug Ressler leaned back in his chair and ran his fingers through his thick grey hair while exhaling. He had been asking himself this same question for the past two months. Staring at the red folder spread open across his desk, he began going over, yet again, its contents in his mind. He nearly had the damn thing memorized by now, from front to back.

That is, of course, until a new homicide is reported in Winsor. And that had been often, far too often for this area. When another one does, he will look over the details and determine whether or not it's related to his case. Like the one last night.

He straightened back up in his seat and pulled out the copy of the homicide report Garrett Johnson worked on. It was Garrett's night to be up, so he took the call when it came in, but Doug almost wished it would have been his turn. Almost. It seemed like all the recent cases could be connected in some way, and if that were true, then more and more people were trampling over his casework. Doug glanced down at the report:

Catherine-Lynn Bobbett, 28 years old, single, lived alone, throat slashed, time of death estimated for 9:13 p.m. The scene of the crime took place in the victim's home, a one-story condo, in a community with twenty-four neighboring units. Across the street from the condominium is a small grocery store by the name of Wrigley's. None of Catherine-Lynn Bobbett's neighbors reported hearing or seeing anything unusual nor did the grocery store's surveillance camera provide anything useful.

Just like the other crime scenes. Was this his man?

Doug huffed and scratched his cheek. The level of stubble was well beyond what he normally wore. He was surprised that none of his fellow detectives had remarked about it yet. But who has time to shave during all this? And does it really matter?

Yes, yes it does. He would need to get his appearance together before he hit the streets again. If the citizens saw him walking around, interviewing neighbors, following up on leads while looking like he just crawled out from a week long Las Vegas drug-binge, they may lose confidence in the city's competence to solve this case. He was already starting to lose confidence in himself. Winsor isn't a large city. The radius is 40.6 square miles with a population of 80, 373. Not a small, rinky-dink town, but not the size of New York either. Not by a long shot. So where the hell was his man? How could someone possibly do all this and not be seen? All within the same area. Winsor has averaged seven murders a year for the past ten years. Last year, they ended with fifteen murders; six of them from October to December. And now, two weeks into the New Year, there was one more. It made *no* damn sense. Doug went back to the crime scene report:

A single, deep slash across the throat with a wide blade. Possibly a hunting knife. Catherine-Lynn Bobbett then died from blood loss after her body went into shock from physical trauma.

Now that was the part that simply didn't add up to Doug. A *single* throat slash? All of the other victims that he could possibly link to the perpetrator died from excessive and brutal physical trauma. Multiple stab wounds, multiple gunshot wounds, multiple contusions and broken bones. All were the results of a violent act taken to extreme lengths; signs of deep rage. Catherine-Lynn's death didn't have any signs of that. The lack of evidence, lack of witnesses and the victim being alone and relatively isolated all matched.

But not the act itself. This one seemed calm, calculated. Was this his man? Or was there another killer in Winsor now? Doug sighed and pinched the bridge of his nose. That was all they needed, another sick bastard out on the loose. It would be much simpler if it was the work of one man, but where the hell was he *hiding*?

"Now since you've been making life much, much easier for Garrett, you're going to do the same for me, right? 'Cause we're best buds and all."

"Hey there, Steve," Doug replied dryly without looking up, "How am I making Garrett's life easy?"

Steve Chandler hovered over Doug's desk, arms crossed in a feigned play of impatience. Though seated, Doug still appeared as the more imposing figure of the two. At 6'3", Steve had a good three inches of height over Doug, but his lanky frame was less threatening than Doug's sturdier 230 weight mass. Doug wasn't built like a weightlifter nor was he soft and doughy. 'Solid' is how the others described him. Steve and Doug had been partners for the past five years and the two worked well together. Steve found himself deferring to Doug's opinion on cases because he felt that he usually picked up on details that Steve overlooked or brushed off as unimportant. It did annoy him slightly that on the street citizens did the same thing; automatically veering toward Doug out of the two, even though Steve was the senior detective. Perhaps it was because he didn't (as of yet) have a lot of grey in his beard or hair. You had to use a microscope, he thought, to find any solid black hairs on Doug's head.

"Oh you know what I mean," Steve remarked, "He catches a

body, you work it for him, he gets to sleep easier." He looked down at the file in Doug's hand. "And there you are proving my point. How many of his bodies are you working right now?"

"Just two, as of now," he mumbled, "they may be linked."

"Yeah, yeah, you should put that on a shirt. Or hang up a plaque on your desk. That's all you've been saying for the past couple months now."

Doug threw Steve a quick, dirty look before turning back to the file. "If there was something else to say, I'd say it." He glanced at his partner again, "Did you stop by here for a reason or was it just to annoy me?"

"A little of both actually," he sat on the edge of the desk, intentionally squashing a few files, "You remember Louis Connelly?"

"Killed in Grey Park, almost five weeks ago. You know I remember. What of it?"

Steve's impish look faded for the first time this night, "After we cased the scene, what did we find?"

"Are we going anywhere with this pointless shit?"

"Just go with it. What did we find?"

Doug sighed again, laced his fingers in front of his belly and did his best to not take over the impish facial expression that Steve had abandoned. "We found Louis alone, recently deceased. Though at the time we didn't know who it was since most of his face was missing. Wallet ID'd him, fingerprints confirmed it. He had been recently arrested for public inebriation. One gunshot wound in his leg, ten more hit his skull, one went into his shoulder. The shoulder wound was probably accidental. Theory is that the leg wound was first to knock him down, then the rest finished him off…Want me to keep going?"

Steve gave a faint smile, "Oh yes, I love it when you talk dirty."

"Fuck off. We went over the entire park with a search team, dogs and metal detectors. No additional evidence was found other than what was on and in the victim's body. We know the caliber of handgun used, a ruger 9mm, but tracing it further than that proved to be a dead-end. All of the recovered rounds had broken apart too much when they hit his bones," Doug paused again and stared at his partner, "I'm waiting for the point of this."

"I wasn't trying to get your hopes up or anything. I merely have an observation I wanted to go over with you." He got off the desk and began pacing around. "Have we checked with the clinics again for any recently released nutcases or escapees?"

"We already checked that and you *know* that's a dead-end. We came up with nothing. Besides," Doug waved his hand over the case files, "none of this seems like the work of someone with mental illness. More like emotional issues, poor anger management."

"Yes I know, but I'm wondering if we're going down the wrong path. You remember Adam Kender? Back in '93?"

Doug closed his eyes and turned his head down slightly. "Kender...yes. Schizophrenic. Lived on Hill Lane. Killed...what was it, twenty-two?"

"Twenty-three, I think."

"Killed twenty-three prostitutes and homeless people over a span of three years. Hid them in his basement and buried some in his backyard. Claimed he 'had to do it' or the voices would rip his brain apart."

"It was already pretty scrambled."

Doug continued, "It was believed that he chose the homeless and sex workers as victims since it would have been less likely for them to be missed. How would their friends and family know they were missing? They're already in exile. Why would the police send out searches for no apparent reason?"

"Exactly."

"And this is the reason why we fought hard against the defense's weak-ass insanity plea. The guy had it too planned out, the victims weren't random. If he was as sick as they claimed he was, he would have shown no selectivity." Doug scratched his beard, "But we lost that one. Jury believed his story, thin as it was, and the judge sentenced him to a hospital for the criminally insane 'for treatment.' After a couple years, if I remember correctly, he ended things with a belt around his neck."

"And no signs of anything sexual," Steve interrupted, "so it was labeled as death by asphyxiation, but nothing more." He glanced off to the side, "This might not be p.c., but I was really hoping he died from a sex thing. Literally caught with his pants down. After all the shit he did, he would've deserved an embarrassment like that."

"Perhaps," Doug mumbled. He gave a long, steady look to his partner, "Why are we bringing up trash like Adam Kender?"

Steve stopped pacing and leaned over the desk again. "Crazy or not, I think our guy might have been treated or diagnosed. I know we looked around for all that already, but we didn't spend enough time on it. I think if we retrace our steps, we can find something there. I'm sure of it."

Doug gave a smile so faint that it went unnoticed by his partner. He loved it when Steve got like this, when he was positive about a lead. When he set his mind on a course like this, he couldn't be dissuaded by anyone or anything until it was resolved. Doug honestly couldn't have asked for a better partner in the entire department, and was glad they both worked so well together.

Unfortunately, he didn't agree with him. Not this time. "Why don't you go on ahead without me on this one? I'll keep poring over these files." He looked back at the red folders and gave an embarrassed smile, "I know I sound like a broken record, man, and I hate leaving you to work that angle alone. But I can't help but feel that these cases are all connected somehow. I feel it in my *gut*. I won't be able to sleep again if I don't figure out how."

Steve had a look of disappointment, but he nodded and gave Doug a pat on the shoulder. "Hey, I understand, no worries." The impish grin returned, "But seriously, if you're trying to push me out of the way so that you and Garrett can run off into the sunset together, you can just say so."

"Quit flirting and get to work, you whore."

Steve laughed and began walking down the hall. Doug shook his head and picked up Allen Carter's file again.

"Hey, Doug?"

He glanced up to see that Steve had stopped walking and was giving him a humorless stare. "We'll catch this guy. It's just a matter of time. You know that, right?"

Doug nodded, "Yeah, I do, I do." He returned the look back at his partner, "Thanks."

Steve turned back around and continued walking. Doug opened up the file in front of him and began reading the interviews from the citizens again. 'Shadow', 'shape' and 'figure' were the consistent descriptions in the report. A shadow, huh? Yeah right. Doug leaned back in his chair and glanced over the wall with the names of all the open murder victims. Too many, far too many of them. Allen Carter wasn't the first, but Doug intended for him to be one of the last. And this figure that everyone's talking about? It wasn't some shadow or specter or a monster.

It was just a man.

Connect

"Life is just another stage. The actors play their parts, the roles are all predetermined. Wouldn't you agree? The only difference between real life and the stage is that we aren't given the scripts ahead of time. And no one tells us that the cameras are rolling."
-----Alexis Ramada

```
     Scene opens on a deserted, rundown house.
Interior and exterior lights are off.  Closest
streetlight is broken.  Weeds and vines are
growing upward on all sides of the house, like
snakes.  A rusty metal fence borders the
house.  Each post is topped with a sharp
spike.  The fence is also covered in vines.
     BRAD:  Are you ready?  There's no turning
back once we go in there.
     ALEXIS:  Are you even sure about this?
How do you know this is the right place?
     B:  We checked the greenhouse and the
factory.  I didn't sense any evil spirits
there.  This is the only other spot around
where the attacks took place.  This must be
it.
     A:  Because that old map we found listed
this as an area of spiritual power.
     B:  For rituals, yes.  These are the only
spots that make sense.
```

"Holy shit, did I really write those lines?"
"Must have, unless somebody else is pretending to be you and turning in these scripts behind your back." Seth raised an eyebrow, "And I'd bet money that isn't happening."

Dylan closed his eyes and pinched the bridge of his nose. He would have been less embarrassed if he showed up on set in his underwear. Or naked. "We've had so many damn rewrites I guess I gave up on making the dialogue work." He looked toward the set and sighed. "As if that wasn't obvious."

"You know," Seth replied, "Alexis really isn't that bad." He added quickly, "Of an actress, I mean. She's a horrible person."

"Oh she's the worst. At least you don't have to deal with her butchering your lines. And lots and *lots* of difficulty with simple terms. Like 'machete.' How do you mispronounce that? She kept saying 'ma-kety.'"

Seth gave a brief laugh. "Tell me someone kept a copy of those takes. I wanna leak that on the internet."

"Get with the editors. They'll have a gold mine for you."

```
B:   You have everything?
A:   Yes, I made sure.  Oh, Jason, I'm so
scared.  Are we going to get out of this
alive?
     Brad grabs Alexis by the arms and turns
her around to face him.  He stares,
heroically, into her eyes.
     B:   Don't you talk that way, dammit!
We'll be fine, both of us.  You hear me,
Mindy?  Your little girl can't grow up without
a mother.  She needs you.
```

"Eww, that was bad. He's *gotta* call 'cut' on that one."

Dylan looked over at Charles sitting in the director's chair. He appeared to be mildly annoyed, but no more than usual and gave no sign of ending the take. "Doesn't seem that way. Guess that one's going to print."

"Eww," Seth repeated.

Alexis looks over the fence in front of them.

A: What is that right there?

Alexis points to a few of the spikes.

A: Is that---

B: It's blood.

Brad stares at the house grimly.

B: Let's hope it has nothing to do with Officer Cole.

A: I don't like this. Not one bit. He was supposed to be here before us.

B: I don't like it either, but what choice do we have? We can't stand out here all night, exposed. We have to go in without him. Carry on with the plan.

Alexis sighs and tightens her grip on the gas can.

A: I won't run away this time. I promise. I'm going to see it through.

"I don't think I know how to write women. What do you think? Is this sexist?"

"Completely," Seth responded without pause, "You should have had her take charge. She just stands around asking questions all the time."

A: Are we climbing over? I don't see an opening.

"See what I mean?"

Brad looks over the fence nervously.

B: I don't see one either. Dammit. We'll have to go over. <u>But be careful</u>. That blood got there somehow.

Alexis slowly climbs over the fence, gas

can in hand. She keeps glancing back from Brad to the house. She gasps when she reaches the top, seeing what is unmistakably blood on top of the spikes.

    A: Jason...

    B: It'll be okay. Keep moving.

Alexis climbs over and reaches the ground unharmed. She sighs when she hits the concrete. Brad throws the travel bag over his shoulder and tightens the strap. He begins climbing over the fence. Once at the top, the sound of rusted metal screeches out and the fence begins to sway.

    A: Look out!!

Before he can react, one of the spikes elongates, magically stretching to the length of a spear and cuts his thigh open.

    B: Dammit!

Brad falls over to the ground and blood starts to spurt from the wound---

"CUT!"

The crew paused and looked over toward Charles. Brad Derk was still holding onto his leg, unsure if he needed to go back to the original marker or stay put. Charles shook his head and paced in front of the camera. "Okay," he yelled, "who the hell is in charge of the blood? Who's pumping it?"

"I am."

Charles whirled around and immediately ripped into Damon. "Why'd the blood come out so late? I didn't see a fuckin' drop until he hit the ground."

Damon glanced around briefly, and then looked at Charles with frank confusion. "Um, I thought I was supposed to begin pumping when he was on the ground. That's what we practiced. I don't remember you ever saying---"

"I've said and I'm *saying* that it needs to happen as soon as we show his leg getting cut. Why the hell wouldn't he bleed then, you idiot? If you can't figure out simple shit like that, then get off my set."

Damon's face turned a deep red and he visibly showed restraint from telling the director where he could shove it. Instead, he politely replied, "Sorry, sir, guess I wasn't thinking. I'll do it right next time."

Charles huffed and shook his head again. "Alright, alright. Places, everyone, back from the top. Yet *again*. And Brad?"

"Yes, Mr. Winston?"

"You're overacting a bit; dial it back. We're not staging a Broadway show, for Christ's sake."

Brad squinted at Charles, but the director didn't catch the look. Alexis Ramada had a thin smile on her face as she moved back to her mark.

"Dylan?"

Dylan turned to see Karen standing close by, smiling warmly. He briefly scrutinized her hair which now appeared to have blue-green streaks in it. "Well hey there, KY! Someone's been a stranger lately. Surprised you even remember my name."

"Oh shut it, you're such a drama queen."

Randy called out from the sidelines, "Quiet on the set, everyone! Everyone, quiet!"

Dylan snickered, "I think that's honestly the one thing that guy does around here." He gave a sidelong glance to Karen, "Think he gets paid more than me?"

"Quiet on the *set!*"

Karen gestured toward the far end of the set and began walking. Once they made it over there, she leaned closer to Dylan's ear, "Are you on break soon? Or do they need you here?"

"No, no, I'm just watching the train wreck. What'd you have in mind?"

"Nothing really," she shrugged, "I just had to get away from that desk before I *killed* somebody."

Dylan smiled, "I hear ya. Well let's do the famous walk 'n' talk and think of something on the way."

  * * * * * * * * * *

"Oh my god, this cold weather is miserable!"

Dylan glanced out the breakroom window. "It's really not that cold."

"I didn't say it was *that* cold; I said the cold is *miserable*. I'd enjoy this much much more if we had some snow."

"Snow? Down here? You better go north a few states if you want that." Dylan absently raised his hand to scratch his hairline and Karen slapped it away, almost by pure reflex. "All we seem to get is icy, mushy dirt. You know, last year I was so desperate for snow that I tried to make snowballs with the ice that fell. Know what I ended up with?"

"What?"

"Wet, dirty hands."

Karen gave a brief laugh, then lightly hit his shoulder. "So you said you were watching the 'train wreck' earlier. Is it really that bad? I honestly have been ignoring the production for the most part. It all just seems the *same*. Like, how many times are we going to make this movie?"

Dylan gave a brief sigh and almost reached his hand up to scratch his hairline again (causing Karen to clench her fists) before he grabbed his lukewarm coffee instead and took a sip. "It's pretty bad," he responded dejectedly, "The dialogue is all over the place. And I know I'm partially to blame for that. It's just that, I don't know, every time I turned around they wanted me to rewrite a scene here, change the location there. I eventually stopped caring and shot pages out quickly because I knew another revision was down the line. They're even ad-libbing some of the lines now, did you know that? Not that I blame them. I cringe, uncontrollably, when I hear them speaking some of those lines out loud. Especially from the 'princess.' "

"Well, can't you make suggestions? I mean, it is your work. If you aren't happy with it, you should try and fix it."

Dylan shook his head slightly and had another sip. "I want it to be over at this point. Tired of hearing about it and people complaining and hearing those freaking *actors* complain about the cameraman getting too close and the director acting like he's making an Oscar contender. It's exhausting. The wrap party may be the only good thing to come out of all this. And that will be 'cause this crap's finally over." He stopped rambling when he realized that Karen was staring at him blankly, reacting to nothing he said. "What?" he asked.

"Sorry, I was waiting for you to tell me how you really felt."

He let out a chuckle and put his coffee down. "Okay, I'll quit whining. It is what it is, right? We all knew what we were getting into when this production started. Same as the ones before. I don't know why I act surprised."

"Oh my god, I know, right? I keep getting aggravated over these stupid horror movies we're doing...and all we do are stupid horror movies. Are we being unrealistic wishing for the studio to do something *different*?"

"Apparently." He looked out the window again. The grey, muted sky greeted him. Winter was more than halfway over, yet it still looked like fall outside. For some reason, this made him think of Allen. Dylan turned back from the window with a somber look, "Okay," he said, "in all seriousness, no bullshit, what's been going on with you lately? You've been missing days of work and I rarely seem to see you when you're here."

She began to speak, then stopped herself. She walked over to the table, sat down and stared at the tabletop for a while. Haltingly she responded, "I've had a lot on my mind. I don't know. I can't stop thinking of Allen. I try and try to work on this stupid movie, but all I see is him. And when I'm home, I think about him trying to walk back from the bar and being alone...and what happened to him." She glanced at Dylan pleadingly, "Is it the same for you?"

He nodded, "Yeah," he stated softly, "Him and Louis, especially at night. I keep having those nightmares."

Karen sighed, "I didn't know Louis. I feel bad about that. I wish I could have talked to him, you know, at least once. Or something. But things got so damn crazy over here...I don't know. I guess that's just an excuse."

"No, no, I understand. You can't get to know everybody. And Louis kept to himself, mostly. He had been having some issues with his wife recently, so he was more withdrawn than usual. He and I were really only close because we went to the same college, but I wouldn't even call us that close. Not really." He looked down at his feet, "I do miss him though."

She nodded quietly and laced her fingers together in front of her. After a minute or so, she broke the silence, "Yeah, so, I've been restless. Like *really* restless for the past three months now. So I've been going out for walks at night. Late night walks, like to clear my head."

He frowned at her. " 'Late night walks?' You know the police issued a city-wide curfew? For everyone. No one's supposed to be out past midnight."

"They're not enforcing it, not for everyone. You know how many businesses would protest? At least the bars. They're closing up a little earlier, at like one or two, but that's it. I've seen the police pick up some teenagers to give them a lift or something. Not much else."

"But *teenagers* aren't the ones getting attacked. At least not yet. And in any case, *you* know about the curfew, whether they are enforcing it or not, and the reason behind it so why the hell are you going out?"

She twiddled her thumbs and pursed her lips at her hands. "You're gonna think I'm crazy," she said, "but I'm actually, kind of, hoping to run into this guy. The killer." Dylan merely stared at her in horror, words escaping him. "I keep a gun on me," she stated quickly, "I picked one up from that gun place, Home Security."

"Wait, you have a license for it? For a gun?"

"Of course I do, how else would I have it? They're so strict now about handing out weapons around here. Which is a *good* thing."

"But," he pinched his nose, "but what are you trying to accomplish? So you have a gun, so what? What does that even mean? You think you're a bounty hunter now?" Karen remained silent and continued to stare at her thumbs. He could tell she was biting the inside of her cheek. "Hey, look, I'm not trying to belittle you or make fun or anything like that. Okay? I just...I just don't understand what you're doing."

She shrugged, "No, it's fine. I wasn't upset. It really doesn't make a lot of sense to me either. I know that it's stupid. Really *really* stupid. But I *can't* sit around doing nothing. It's driving me crazy. Every time I'm sitting in my apartment, every time I'm walking to my car, every time I'm not around a lot of people I'm a hot mess. Just nervous as all hell. Like, if I look over my shoulder at the right moment, that psycho will be there behind me." He pushed the coffee away and sat next to her. He didn't say anything yet; waiting for her to finish. "So I get the great idea of getting a gun," she continued, "Pretty smart, right? Solves all the world's problems. But the funny thing is, I actually *did* feel better just having it. I don't know if I could ever use it when it came down to it. Probably couldn't, but at least I felt better." She paused and bit her cheek again, "But something was still off, something still felt like it was missing." She finally looked up from her hands and stared hard into his eyes. "So I started going on these walks, all the time. By myself."

"But why would you do that?"

"Because I want to kill that sonofabitch myself."

Dylan leaned back from her, mouth agape. He couldn't even guess how to respond to that statement. She stated it so frankly and clearly that there was no doubt she was being completely honest about it. She stared at him, waiting for his response and didn't seem inclined to continue until he remarked. "Karen," he stammered, "I don't...how can you..." he cleared his throat and tried again, "You realize that's a death wish, don't you? It's suicidal."

She shook her head, "I'm not suicidal and that's not what this feels like. Not at all. It may not be smart---well, it's actually really goddamn far from that, but I feel like I'm doing something. And who knows, maybe I'll be the one to take him down."

He got up and began to pace by the window, hands on hips. Unconsciously, he mimicked her by biting his cheek, instead of scratching his hairline. He stopped and looked outside at all the dead leaves on the grass. The faint, rotten stench came back to his nostrils. "Okay," he said after letting out a deep breath, "this is what we're going to do: You're going to allow me to install one of those cellphone tracking apps on your phone." He raised his hand, "Let me finish. We're going to install it so that when you go on these walks, I can be close by. Not right next to you, in case you're...well, worried of me scaring off this creep. I'll be a block over or something. And on your phone, you're going to have my number brought up so that if anything happens, you can just push one button and I'll be right over."

" 'Be right over' with what? You have a gun too?"

"No, I'll...I'll either get one too or think of something else. Don't worry about that part."

"Dylan, you don't need---"

"*No*," he replied sternly, cutting her off, "I don't care if this upsets you or pisses you off, but I'm going to do this with you. I won't be able to sleep at all if I think you're out there walking around alone. So I might as well do something if I'm going to be up anyway, alright?" He paused briefly, "So don't fight me on this, okay? Just let me come with you."

Karen smiled for the first time since they briefly mentioned snow. "Fine," she stated, "but I don't want you installing any porn on my phone when you put that app on there. I know how bored you screenwriters get."

He gave a half-smirk and followed her lead. "I promise to be a perfect gentleman while I'm messing around with your phone. Don't worry. I may even get a call back."

"And if we do catch this guy, I want to be the one that talks to the cops and reporters. Your nervous, balding ass will make me look bad."

"You know there are times, like right now, when I really hate your honesty."

      *   *   *   *   *   *   *   *   *

```
     Alexis looked around her in a panic.  The
smoke from the flames was beginning to fill
the hallway.  The doors on both ends were
still locked and shut tight.  Brad was beating
one of the doors with a crowbar, but the wood
remained undamaged.  It seemed to have a
protective magic barrier.  Brad starts to kick
the doors and throws the crowbar down.
     B:  Dammit, dammit, dammit!  It can't end
like this!  You hear me?!  It can't!
     A:  Jason?  Jason.
Brad continues to kick the door and yell.
     A:  Jason!
Brad turns back toward her.
     A:  What are we going to do?  What can we
do?
```

Brad looks back at the door. Flames are starting to come in from the sides and bleed onto the walls. Brad's shoulders slump and he walks back over to Alexis. He sits on the ground next to her feet.

    A: No, we can't give up! There must be another exit. A window! There has to be one.

    B: There isn't, we checked.

    A: Well let's check again! Maybe we missed it. Maybe it's---

    B: Mindy, it's over. There's no way out. The evil spirits weren't fighting us because they knew we would be trapped in here, those rotten bastards. I should have known it was going too smoothly. When we lit the first fire, I should have known.

    A: But, but we---

    B: It's over, we won.

Brad gives a weak smile and holds his hand out to Alexis.

    B: There may be no way out for us, but it's the same for this house. It can't stop what we've done. It's going to die with us. No one else will get hurt. We saved everyone.

Alexis looks at his hand, then she takes it, sits down next to him and wraps her arm around his torso. Brad leans his head against hers and they both watch as the flames spread across the walls, getting closer and closer---

"Wait, hold on, I'm confused. Can we cut here? Is that okay?"

Charles let out a brief growl, and then yelled, "Cut!" He got out of his chair and slowly walked toward Alexis. "Confused about what, my dear? What could possibly be confusing about this scene?"

She waved a hand toward the fake doors. "Well, where are the flames supposed to be? I don't know what we're supposed to be looking at and we don't have any markers showing us."

"We don't have time for any of that, this scene needs to get done today and I gave you very simple directions. I just said look slowly from the doors, to the front of you and back. By the time you sit down, the flames are basically everywhere."

"Well that doesn't help us at all. Right, Brad?"

Brad quickly glanced at Charles, then back to Alexis. "Um, I, well," he gave another glance to the director, "I wasn't having any issues with the scene."

"We both need clearer instructions," she stated, ignoring her co-star, "and can you tell your cameraman to move back some? I can't concentrate on my lines when he's right over me."

Charles glowered at her; the pure rage pouring from him seemed to be physically felt by everyone on the set. Everyone that is, except for Alexis Ramada. She continued to wait, bright-eyed, for him to answer her. After staring at her for two full minutes, Charles turned his back on her and faced the crew. "Alright, everybody," he stated in a calm but powerful voice, "let's break for now and return in an hour. We have some things we need to get *situated*."

The crew dispersed with some heading to the break areas and others moving to the sides of the set to converse. Brad and Alexis both left the set together and both would probably be late when it was time for the cameras to roll again. That was a daily occurrence. "Mr. Winston, can we talk for a moment?" a voice called out.

Charles turned and frowned at the head screenwriter, Dylan Haddon, standing a few feet from him. "This sure as hell better not be any more bad news," he replied, "I've had enough of all you today."

Dylan let out a small cough and scratched his hairline. "Uh, hopefully you don't see it that way. I think it's a good thing, actually." He paused briefly, "I want to do another rewrite of this scene. Would only be a few lines of dialogue, but I think it would make a world of difference."

Charles frown became more severe. "Are you high? You're bringing this shit up now? On the last shooting days? You've got to be kidding."

Dylan shook his head, "No, sir, I mean it. This scene had been bugging me more than the others, but I couldn't figure out why. I just got finished talking to one of my co-workers when it finally hit me: It's the *logic* of the scene. Not the dialogue or the action, though those have their own issues. But the logic behind the scene is weak, frankly, and it hurts the characters."

Charles huffed, "Pal, *no one* gives a shit about the logic, okay? This is a horror movie. A low budget, cable T.V. one at that. Maybe a few dozen people will watch it other than us. And those people just want to see a few deaths, a couple jump-scares, and as much blood as we can get away with. Then they move on, that's it. So let's get this shot and done and not overthink it." He turned to walk away, but stopped when he heard Dylan speak up again.

"I just want to change the decision behind their deaths. They look like complete idiots at the end, getting caught in their own trap. And I'm as much to blame for the scene as anyone. Or more so since I wrote it, so I'd like to fix it. If they're going to get caught, I want it to be on purpose. They *want* that to happen. It's the only way they found to beat this---" he waved his hand out, "*thing* that's taken over their town. The only way to make it go away."

Charles had continued to stare at Dylan, but his features had softened considerably. "Do you have the slightest idea yet on what to change and how?"

"Yes, sir," he said while pointing to his forehead, "I'm already working it out. Shouldn't even take half an hour to fix."

"Do it then. I want the revised pages within the hour. And don't change the fucking color for the revision. I think we ran the hell out of colors."

    Dylan gave a thin smile, a small nod and began walking back to his office. He felt that things were, finally, falling into place for the production.

The Man

An animal, a beast
Destructive, consuming
Selfish and deluded
Other lives are others' concerns
A monster, a shadow
A man

The man sat and contemplated the wall.

He stared at it and let his mind wander over a range of subjects. How long had this building stood here? How long should he stay here? Why was he so restless and tired? Why was he so angry?

In his right hand, he held a pocket knife with a six inch blade. With it, he was deliberately cutting grooves into the floor. It began as an organized, linear series, but became progressively scattered and messy the further he worked on it.

He also thought about what he should do with the knife. It was becoming more and more of a chore to clean up after himself. More work. And much more aggravation. The simplicity was gone. So much more work. More, more, *more*.

He flung the knife across the room in a flash of movement. It embedded itself a third of the way into the opposite wall. His arm tingled from the surprising movement and his heartbeats pounded in his ears. He grasped the floor, then scraped his dirty fingernails across the surface until his hands became tightly wound fists.

He unclenched them, then tightened them again. Unclenched, clenched. His heartbeat continued to pound throughout his head. Faster than before.

A squeak emitted from across the room. He turned his head towards the sound. He detected no movements. He continued to stare, waiting. Subconsciously, he halted his breathing.

The squeak came again, then a slight movement. In the corner of the room, a mouse was sniffing the floor boards. Its whiskers going up and down as its small nose hunted for food.

The man began to breathe again. His eyes flicked over to the knife stuck in the wall. He shifted his eyes back to the mouse again. Not far at all. He slowly rose to his feet and took a small step toward the wall. The mouse stopped its search and raised its ears. He waited. The mouse looked toward him, and then peered around the room. Minutes passed.

Eventually, the mouse's nose resumed its search and the whiskers began dancing again. The man took another step. Then another. The mouse briefly halted its search, then continued. Clearly considering the room safe from harm.

After three more steps, the man had reached the knife. He loosened it from the wall, causing bits of paint and plaster to sprinkle the floor. He turned back to the mouse and saw it had gained some distance from him. Still hunting, but now at a more frantic pace.

The man stood still. One, two, three, fou---

In a series of movements that seemed contradictory to his bulky build, he leapt across the room, brought the knife down with all of his strength, plunged it straight through the mouse and buried it deep into the wooden floor underneath. Only the hilt was visible; the blade had disappeared all the way into the mouse's body.

The mouse's leg twitched and a bit of blood dripped from its nose, adding to the little pool it now laid in.

The pounding in the man's head had stopped. His breathing became less labored. He unclenched his fists and his hands hung limply at his sides. Once again, he was calm.

It always made him calm.

The Figure, pt. 2

    Dylan opened his eyes and knew immediately that something wasn't quite right.

    He was standing outside on a long stretch of grasslands that went out as far as he could see. Nimbus clouds blanketed the sky and flashed from occasional lightning. A single tree, a hundred yards away, was the only object in the strange field.

    "Do you see? What I've come to see?"

    Dylan spun around. Directly behind him was Karen, in a dark blue dress. Her hair was a red so dark that he could only tell that it wasn't black when the lightning flashed. "Do you see?" she asked. She looked at him sadly and searched his face for a sign of understanding. Rain droplets began falling from the sky. He watched, transfixed, as the rain left red streaks down her face. He thought the rainwater was mixing with her hair coloring, but then he looked down at his arms and saw the red streaks appearing on them. "Do you see?"

    He gazed up at the clouds. "I see the sky raining blood," he replied. Slowly, Karen lifted one of her arms and pointed to a spot behind him. He looked back over his shoulder. Under the tree, there now stood a shadow. A gaping blackness in the form of a human. The shadow had its arms extended to the sides with the palms face up. Pools of blood were forming and spilling out from those palms. Bright red trails ran down the length of the shadow's arms and colored its sides like paint.

    Karen walked past Dylan and headed toward the shadow. "Karen?" he called out. She kept walking. He reached out to her, "Karen!" She kept walking away, never acknowledging his calls. She was suddenly very close to the shadow, its arms reaching for her.

Dylan lunged forward to run after her and lost his footing. And then he fell. The ground disappeared underneath and an infinite darkness, a void, opened up to swallow him whole. He grasped desperately around him as he tumbled through the air. He called out Karen's name again and again during his descent, but his voice no longer had the power to reach her.

* * * * * * * * *

Dylan sat up in bed and grabbed at his chest. His heart was pounding very fast and very strongly. *That was a bad one*, he thought, *Never had one with Karen in it before.* He threw off the blanket, swung his legs over the side and let the ceiling fan cool him down. His sheets were damp with sweat. He glanced over at the alarm clock, 8:29 a.m. He needed to be at the office in half an hour. He rubbed his eyes and walked into his bathroom to start getting ready.

In the middle of brushing his teeth, he paused and went back to a thought he had earlier. *Never had one with Karen in it before...* He went over to the night table, grabbed his cellphone and dialed Karen's number. It immediately went to voicemail. *Is she still asleep?* *Beep* "Hey, Karen, it's Dylan. I was just calling to check up on you. I guess I'll see you at the office? Talk to you later, bye." He hung up, went to put the phone down, then thought better of it and sent her a text as well.

After he pulled into his parking spot at the studio, he checked his phone again. Still no reply. He tried calling her and once more he got the voicemail. He frowned, then got out of the car and headed off toward the receptionist's desk. The halls were bustling with activity. People were scurrying in and out like chickens. The production on the film officially ended today and everyone was trying to finish early to get ready for the wrap party tonight. Dylan squeezed through the crowd and stepped into Lindsay's office. "Hey there, Lin, good morning."

Lindsay Davidson was in her late twenties with shoulder length, straight brown hair. Black rimmed eyeglasses complimented her features and she always wore dark or muted colors for her business attire. She flashed him a quick smile and went back to her computer screen. "Hey, Dylan, things are kind of crazy right now."

He looked back over his shoulder, "Yeah, I can tell," he turned back to her, "Look, I don't mean to bug you, but can you tell me if Karen checked in? Or if she called earlier?"

"Karen Young?" she pressed a few keys on the keyboard, "Hmm, yeah I'm showing she called around 8:00 this morning, said she wouldn't be in today. 'Would try to make the party.' " Dylan's gaze was focused on a point somewhere above Lindsay's head and remained there as he replayed her words. "Was there...anything else?"

He returned his gaze to her and forced a smile that didn't reach his eyes. "No," he said calmly, "that's exactly what I needed. Thank you." He started to walk out, and then turned back halfway. "Um, if anyone is searching for me, tell them I'll be back later. I need to take care of something."

"Oh, okay, sure. When should I tell them you'll be back? Around what time?"

Dylan raced out the door and hurried down the hall. He didn't attempt to answer her. Once outside, he loaded up the new app on his phone that linked to Karen's. The signal searched and pinpointed her phone's location to the southern edge of town, close to where Winsor turned into Evangeline. He felt a cold tightness hit his stomach as he stared at the beacon. Then jumped in his car and began driving toward the signal.

Once within two hundred feet of where the signal was being sent, he slowed down and surveyed the neighborhood. It was a rural area, with long stretches in-between the houses. The trees were small and lanky, but numerous. The condition of the houses was inconsistent. Some were pristine and seemed ready for sale, while others were in varying states of disrepair.

Dylan slowed to a stop and looked in the rearview mirror at the object that caught his attention. He put the car in reverse and backed up next to a car that was parked on the side of the road. The car looked exactly like Karen's. The coldness struck again and nearly clenched his stomach shut. He grabbed the phone off the dashboard and dialed a number.

"911," a voice answered, "What is your emergency?"

"I need to speak to the lead detective working the series of murders that started around the fall."

"That would be detective Ressler. And is this an emergency?"

"Yes it is," Dylan replied while turning off his car and climbing out, "I think I may know where he can find his suspect." He started jogging toward Karen's cellphone signal, "And I think a couple police cars need to be sent to the address I'm about to give you. *Quickly*. I'm very certain that something horrible was happened."

* * * * * * * * *

When he arrived at the house, he cursed himself fiercely. He realized that he forgot to pick up some sort of weapon before he got here. *Too late now*, he thought, *should I wait?* He wasn't sure how long it was going to take for the police to show up. He looked down the street and listened for sirens. The street was very quiet; he didn't even hear the typical barking of dogs.

He turned back to the house. Its walls were a weather-worn peach color. The window frames were a bright blue that clashed and stood out. The trim and door frame were an eggshell white. None of the colors worked together, but other than that the house appeared to be relatively normal. And quiet. *But Karen may be in trouble in there.* There was no mistake that her cellphone was inside that house; anything else was a guess. He couldn't wait, not if she needed his help. He took a deep breath and walked up to the entrance.

He carefully tried the doorknob and the door swung open effortlessly. He scrunched up expecting the door to creak loudly, but it barely made a sound. He stared into the interior for a few moments. There was no one by the entrance or the nearby stairway. A narrow hallway lead toward what appeared to be a dining area. He took a few steps in, very conscious of his breathing and how loud his heartbeat seemed to be. There was an area immediately to his left, perhaps a living room, completely void of furniture. He took a couple more steps and looked up the stairwell. No lights were on and the top of the stairs were encased in shadows.

He held his breath and listened for any sort of noise. He couldn't pick up anything apart from his heart. He creeped down the hall to the next room. The door was ajar and it was also an empty, furniture-less room. Suddenly the air felt thick and heavy with moisture and there was a smell in the air that Dylan couldn't quite pinpoint. He knew he had smelled it before, but he couldn't focus. The smell made him think of iron. He walked down to the next room in the hallway. The door was halfway open and the smell seemed to be stronger from here. He raised his hand and lightly pushed the door open. A small creak issued from the hinges.

The first thing he saw was a broken window, glass completely shattered but still held together within the frame. At the center where the cracks seemed to be spread out from was a dark red stain. Before he could guess what it was, he looked down and noticed the body on the floor. And then he realized what that smell was. Blood was spread out in a large pool from the body. The body was face-up with its head turned to the side. Dylan stopped breathing. "Oh god no," he whispered, "don't be her. Please don't be her." He stepped around the blood and bent over to get a clearer view of the body's features.

The face was covered in blood and dyed hair, but there was

no mistake it was Karen. He could see one of her eyes and her cheek in-between the hair. That blue-green streaked hair that he meant to comment upon, but never did. He drew in a sharp breath and bit his tongue; he had almost cried out her name. She had been stabbed multiple times in the chest. He didn't need to check for a pulse or look for respiration to know there wasn't any.

"God damn it," he said, unable to contain it, "why didn't you call me?" He stepped into the blood, kneeled down next to her and placed his hand on her cheek. She felt so cold and sickly, he almost pulled back immediately, but forced himself to leave his hand there. He felt his eyes begin to water and he started to say something else, perhaps a goodbye or an apology, when he heard a floorboard creak behind him.

He froze, forcing even his heart to stop, and listened. The creak came again from the hallway, close to the front door. Dylan turned back to Karen's body and patted her front pockets. Not there. He strained and lifted her right side up from the ground; his hands became soaked immediately. He reached around and patted her lower back. Under her shirt, he felt it. He pulled it out from her waistband and stared at it briefly. Her handgun. He tightened his blood-soaked hand around it, flipped the safety and walked out into the hallway. He turned toward the door and looked right at the figure standing nearby blocking the path. It was a bulky form, dressed in all black clothing and a black mask. The light coming in from the doorway behind outlined it well enough that Dylan could tell it was a man. Just a man in an outfit.

They stared at each other for a few moments. Dylan glanced down and saw that the man held a box cutter in his right hand, fully extended. He looked back up at the mask; it was noticeable expanding and contracting with the man's breathing. Then the man tilted his head to the side and turned halfway to the door. Dylan heard it too; off in the distance but getting considerably louder were sirens. Police sirens.

"They're coming," Dylan stated dryly, "I called them before I walked in. They know you're here." He bared his teeth with a sneer, "It's over."

The man turned his head back toward him and became still. Then a voice came out from the mask, surprising Dylan in its clarity, "I guess I better hurry then." Then in a flash of speed, the man leapt forward and charged at him. Dylan jumped back, lifted the gun and fired two shots before he was tackled and knocked to the ground. The man had a gloved hand pressing down on Dylan's face, pushing it into the floorboards with great force. Then a sharp piercing pain hit him right underneath the ribs and he cried out. Dylan felt his left lung contract and looked down to see the box cutter buried in his side. The man pulled the blade out, then swept his arm down to stab him again. Dylan lifted the gun up and fired point-blank into the man's chest. The man paused, swayed a bit, and then raised the blade again. Dylan fired two more times and the man fell back and crashed onto the ground.

Dylan groaned as he sat up and crawled over to the sprawled out body. He put his free hand on the mask and pulled it off of the face underneath. Piercing green eyes, jet-black hair and lean features greeted him. Dylan looked over the face for some defining characteristic; a scar, a lazy eye, anything out of the ordinary. But there wasn't one. The face was plain, forgettable. It was just a regular man.

"Why?" Dylan hissed. He placed the gun barrel under the man's chin and forced him to stare into his eyes. "*Why?*" he repeated, "Tell me why. I need you to tell me *why.*"

"Why act surprised?" the man responded in a monotone with a slight gurgle in his words. "You've seen all this play out," he continued, "so many times before." Then the man smiled, and Dylan pulled the trigger before he realized it. Blood splashed his face and got into his eyes, blinding him. He could hear the man choking, still breathing. He fired the gun again, and again, and again. Until he couldn't hear the breathing anymore, until he couldn't hear the gunshots anymore.

He couldn't hear anything over the sound of his own screams.

Leaves

"...We'll catch this guy. You know that, right?"
----Steve Chanlder

"How's he doing?'

One of the paramedics glanced over at Doug, "We stopped the bleeding and patched him up, but we need to get him over to the hospital. The wound was fairly deep and we can't be certain to the extent of the internal damage."

Doug nodded, "I understand. I'll take him over there." Both paramedics turned back to him with confusion. "It'll be okay, I promise to get him there quickly." He looked down at Dylan and held out his hand, "You ready to go, kid?" Dylan leaned forward to stand up and let out a low groan. Doug reached under his shoulder, grabbed his elbow and helped him to his feet. "Come on, car's right over here."

Dylan grimaced and walked stiffly to the car. Doug helped him into the back, and then got into the driver's seat. "What hospital did they say? St. Michael's?" Silence greeted him from the backseat. "Yeah, it must be Michael's," he stated while pulling onto the street, "Closest one." After a few moments, Doug spoke up again, knowing that he was mostly talking to himself. "What a mess. Such a horrible, horrible mess," he shook his head, "It shouldn't have turned out like this."

"You wanted him to live?"

Doug paused before he responded, surprised to hear Dylan's voice, "I don't know. I honestly don't. Jail might not have made any difference. Guy clearly had a lot of issues. But I didn't wish for him to die; I don't wish that on anybody. If he wasn't so violent and angry...why are some people always so *angry*?" He shook his head and glanced in the rearview mirror, "I'm sorry we didn't get here sooner, son. That we--that *I* didn't track him down. I promise you I tried." He glanced in the rearview again and saw that Dylan wasn't reacting to anything he was saying, simply staring at the back of the seat in front of him, blankly.

Doug drove in silence for a while, berating himself again for his initial reaction at the scene. When he got the call, he was hopeful but still filled with skepticism. Could it really be over? Did they actually get his man? Then he arrived at the scene and saw Steve, who was already getting information from the first responders. As soon as Doug turned his car off, Steve walked over and, without a hint of irony or humor, stated, "It's him. It's closed."

"You sure?"

"Completely." Then Steve placed his hand on Doug's shoulder and allowed a hint of a smile to come through.

Doug turned toward the house. "And he's dead?"

"Yeah. Hope he fucking rots."

Doug felt a small flash of disappointment, and it filled him with shame. He should have been glad that it was over, that the killer was dead. It was just that he hadn't wanted it to end like this. He had wanted to chase this man down himself, wanted to catch him and slap the bracelets on his wrists. Wanted to be the escort that brought him to jail and to be there when the court laid down the sentence. Only after the judge stated the verdict and after he saw this son of a bitch go away for a long, long time would he have felt it was worth it. That the work they did was worth it. But this? Did he spend all those sleepless nights to be *late*? For his perp to be killed and not live out his remaining, miserable years in a cell? And to have yet another victim under his belt before he died as well?

"I didn't want anyone else to die," Doug said aloud, breaking away from his reminiscing, "I'm just *sick* of all the death."

Dylan finally stirred behind him and looked out the side window. "It was inevitable, I suppose. Karen and I should have guessed that. We should have known better."

"How do you mean?"

Dylan shrugged and turned to meet Doug's gaze in the

rearview mirror. "Do you remember the last time you saw fireflies, detective? How long it's been since they were around? I was thinking about that the other day."

"Fireflies?" He pursed his lips in thought, "Can't say that I do. It has been a long time, hasn't it? I wonder if they all died out."

It was a couple of minutes before Dylan responded. "They're so small and delicate," he said, "and everything is so rough and cruel around us. I don't think their fragile little bodies can survive in this world. Not anymore. It's simply too dark for their lights to do any good."

They drove in silence for the rest of the trip, while behind them the leaves that littered the street were tossed into the air; twisting and tumbling, before coming back down scattered in the wake of their departure.

Epilogue

Spring would eventually return to the city of Winsor. Until then, the leaves will rot on the cold, frozen earth.

Printed in Great Britain
by Amazon